BEHIND CLOSED DOORS

A DETECTIVE INSPECTOR TAYLOR CASE-FILE

PHILLIP JORDAN

FIVE FOUR PUBLISHING

Surjit,

I hope you enjoy
the book!

P. Ju—

Get Exclusive Material

**GET EXCLUSIVE NEWS AND UPDATES FROM THE
AUTHOR**

Thank-you for choosing to read this book.

Sign-up for more details about my life growing up on the same streets that Detective Inspector Taylor treads and get an exclusive e-book containing an in-depth interview and a selection of True Crime stories about the flawed but fabulous city that inspired me to write, *all for free.*

Details can be found at the end of **BEHIND CLOSED
DOORS.**

Chapter 1

"There's no clock in here."

It was an accurate observation. The absence of a clock meant there was no way to pinpoint and measure the passage of time and served to ratchet up the acute anxiety Jimmy Harding was feeling.

He slammed a balled fist against the thick plexiglass panel of a door that had no lock yet couldn't be opened. The door remained unyielding.

"I need to know about Julie! Is she OK? For God's sake, tell me something!" he shouted.

He slammed his fist home again, half-heartedly this time. Resting his head against the opaque glass, tears fell down his face.

"You can't keep me locked in here not knowing." He slumped against the door and rubbed the heels of his hands into his eyes. "Please, what about wee Tommy? He wasn't breathing. Jesus, he wasn't breathing."

Jimmy stalked across the room. He stared at the beady black eye set in the wall at head height above the only other furniture in the room. A table and four chairs. Ensconced in the smooth dry-lined ceiling, covered panel lights hummed overhead.

"Can you hear me?"

He looked into the lens. Red eyed, hair askew and hanging on his last ragged nerve.

Chapter 2

Detective Inspector Veronica Taylor scanned the charge sheet and glanced up at the large screen that dominated the wall of the observation suite and displayed Interview Room 3.

"Jesus, he wasn't breathing."

The voice captured by the AKG boundary microphones in the Interview Room was relayed in total clarity through the FAP-40T in-ceiling loudspeakers above her head. The voice that filled the observation suite was strained and creaked on the verge of breakdown.

"I still can't see why they dragged you in? I'm perfectly capable of handling something like this myself. It's hardly one for bloody Inspector Morse, is it?"

Taylor ignored the comment from the man standing behind her. She confirmed that at least the initial paperwork was in order, which was something. The suspect's face loomed in the screen.

"Can you hear me?"

Taylor slipped the charge sheet into the document folder on the desk beside the mixing equipment and the digital video and voice recorders that monitored the room next door.

"Where's DI MacDonald again?" she said.

"Majorca," said Samuel Simpson. Resentment that his DI

was sunning himself in the Balearics while he remained stuck in an unseasonably wet and miserable Belfast was evident in his tone. His body language suggested that having his interview gate-crashed was also an affront to an equal power.

Taylor looked at her watch and then to the subordinate officer leaning nonchalantly against the door frame.

If CID didn't work out for him, he'd be a good snake oil salesman. Detective Constable Samuel Simpson liked to believe that his nickname, Slick, was due to his sharp dress sense and the suave sophistication he reserved for superiors and colleagues of the opposite sex.

Taylor knew, however, that behind his back any self-respecting WPC and her own Detective Sergeant Robert Macpherson put it down to his egregious oiliness and the half tub of hair ointment that slicked his hair into a style he thought gave him a debonair look.

"Well, have you read enough?" Simpson pointed at the document folder. His enthusiasm to impress those further up the chain of command did not extend to her.

"Yes. I think it's time Mr Harding explained his version of events."

Simpson scoffed. He smoothed his narrow spotted tie and adjusted the ostentatious pin that held it in place.

"What's to explain? Creep shot his wife and child. Had the gun on him when he was lifted and kept telling anybody who would listen that he was sorry. No brainer, Veronica."

Taylor pursed her lips.

"Guv will do, DC Simpson. Make sure any additional reports from the scene or the hospital are legible and accurate when I ask for them. Can you manage that?"

Simpson glowered and then took a seat at the recording console. He hitched up his skinny-fit suit trousers to reveal an inch of sun-bed tanned leg and paisley patterned socks.

"I still don't see why they dragged you in. This is a hole-in-one." Simpson tossed a biro onto his spiral notepad.

Taylor tightened the bobble and pulled her shoulder-length chestnut hair into a sleek ponytail.

"It's tunnel vision like that got me involved, Slick," she said. "No-one wants your lazy thinking turning this into an albatross around our necks."

Chapter 3

Detective Sergeant Doc Macpherson's face was flushed and his teeth were bared in a grimace resembling a snarling bear. This was odd considering his moniker derived from his uncanny likeness to one of Snow White's famous friends.

"Jesus, I'm sweating like a priest in a primary school. Here, Tinkerbell. Pull this bloody suit off me."

Detective Constable Erin Reilly shook her head in dismay at the spectacle. The battle to extricate himself from the clinging Tyvek oversuit was more akin to wrestling an angry octopus than the simple task it should have been.

She stowed her used suit, her overshoes, and finally her nitrile gloves in the boot of the pool Vauxhall.

"You want to cut down on the sausage rolls, Sarge. It'd be easier cutting you out of this."

"You're a cheeky wee witch, Erin."

"Call it as I see it."

Macpherson blew a long breath as he was finally freed. He groaned as he bent to pluck off his blue overshoes.

"You can't fatten a thoroughbred," he said, nodding sagely as Reilly held open a paper bag for him to deposit the plastic shoe covers into.

"Or a mongrel." Her eyes sparkled with mirth. Gymnastlithe and sharp as a whip, all five foot five of her was a bundle of excited energy. With her enthusiasm, ever-present toothy smile and pixie cut, it looked like she was barely out of school. A mistake Reilly could rectify with her acerbic wit and a look that Macpherson had seen only once and determined never to have visited on him again.

"That's some day."

It was. In the sense that it was something awful. The wind whipped across an expanse of open farmland broken only by the wicked spines of a hawthorn bush and the rickety fence that surrounded the property but did little to protect it from element or intruder. Rainwater glugged as the gutters and downspouts attempted to carry the deluge of a brief but violent shower from the roof to the overflowing drains, the greedy mouths of which were covered in a moult of slimy autumn leaf.

"God, that's gone cold." Reilly winced as she swallowed the dregs of a coffee.

"Not as cold as that wee soul."

Macpherson had slid into the passenger seat. He pulled a bag of sticky pear drops from the glove box, his eyes on the blacked out undertaker's van pulling out of the driveway.

"What possessed him?" said Reilly, tipping the last of the coffee onto the pebbled drive.

Macpherson looked up at the house. Every window was illuminated by lamplight and she could see the stirring of strangers within.

It would have been a peaceful scene a few hours ago. The glow of Belfast City and glimpse of the Lough as you approached over the hill in the late afternoon light. Nice winding country lane. A house of whitewashed stone. A pretty country cottage with a rough pebble drive and slightly overgrown lawn. A simple hand-tooled sign on the gate: 'White Cottage'. A wooden playhouse atop a climbing frame and swings plopped in the centre of the grass with a well-trodden path leading from the side stable door to the old outhouses set further back in a wildflower meadow.

Now, though, it was a crime scene.

Chapter 4

"Are they OK? Is my son all right?" Jimmy Harding had aged ten years in the two hours he had been in custody. He sucked at a bloody rag nail, then rapidly changed tack to chew the skin at the edge of his index finger.

"If you could take a seat, Mr Harding." Veronica Taylor gestured to the seat. A smile and nod.

Harding swept his fingers through his hair, giving them a break from the feasting. The sleeve of his grey sweatshirt rode up to reveal red scratches on his wrist and forearm.

"Can you…" His voice died away as Taylor shook her head.

"Please. Take a seat and a deep breath."

"Mr Harding, the inspector needs you to calm down and take…" The duty solicitor jerked back in his chair as the enraged face turned on him.

"Calm down! Calm fucking down! I need to know if my son is dead and neither of you are telling me a damn thing!" The bitten finger waved between Taylor and the brief, Harding's ire rising in waves.

Taylor pulled out her own chair and sat, unfazed. She'd seen it all before. There was a knock at the door, followed by a series of short beeps. Harding's attention strayed. A nervous twitch, expecting perhaps the heavy mob. The door opened and a woman entered wearing a high street skirt suit and sensible flats, a tablet under her arm. She smiled, even though the tension was treacle thick.

"This is Detective Constable Cook. She'll be sitting in. Mr Harding, please. If you'll just sit, then we can get started and get you up to speed."

Harding dropped into the chair. The adrenaline of his arrest and the fight for news cut from under him. His arms dropped to his sides. He stared at the ceiling, a tear escaping the corner of his eye, which he wiped away.

The duty solicitor rearranged his notebook to make right angles with the desk and swapped the pen in his hand for one in his pocket.

Taylor waited a second, allowing a moment for all to compose themselves and for Simpson to prepare, note the time and ensure the system was recording.

The dual tone was clear when it sounded. Flat, then a higher pitch.

"Interview commences at 7:47 P.M. Present in the room, Detective Inspector Veronica Taylor, Detective Constable Carrie Cook and…"

"Henry Scott, solicitor for Mr Harding."

"And?"

Harding was a million miles away.

"Could you state your name, please, Sir," said Taylor.

"Jimmy…. James Harding."

"Thank you. Jimmy, we've arrested you for the incident that took place this afternoon at 179 Dunregan Road, Belfast, contrary to the Firearms Order of 2004. Do you understand?"

"What about Julie? And Tommy?" said Harding. He was nodding but not listening. He sat up, seeking an answer.

Taylor looked him square in the eye.

"Jimmy, your wife is in theatre. The prognosis isn't good and by the time the night is out there's every likelihood you'll be facing serious charges in connection with her injuries and possibly even her death."

Harding didn't blink. No emotion registered on his face. Beside her, Cook shuffled in her seat and crossed her ankles under the chair.

"Your son, Tommy." Taylor slid a six-by-eight glossy image of a farmhouse kitchen from the document wallet in front of her and flipped it around so Harding and Scott could take in the aftermath. Better to have it up close and in their face rather than put up on the wall-mounted hi-res monitor. A picture from Country Home and Garden, it wasn't.

"Tommy died at the scene, Jimmy. I'm sorry for your loss but I have to inform you we are now re-arresting you for assault occasioning actual bodily harm. We expect that the PPS will pursue a charge of murder. DC Cook?"

Cook pushed the formal paperwork across to the solicitor, whose face had blanched as the chain of misery Harding had unleashed wrapped tighter around him.

Taylor had seen plenty of tougher men than Harding dissolve when faced with the prospect of life imprisonment. What she hadn't expected was for him to resign himself so quickly. He looked at the image, reached out, then retracted his hand as though stung.

"...do say can be used as evidence? Do you understand?" said Cook.

Jimmy Harding sighed and sat back.

"I'm sorry," he said.

"Do you understand the reason you've been arrested and your rights as DC Cook has read them to you?" asked Taylor.

"Yes. Yes I do. I didn't mean to do it."

"That's OK. We'll come to that. We'll give you a few minutes to compose yourself and consult your solicitor. Would you like another room, Mr Scott?"

"This is fine, Inspector. It would seem my client wishes to

assist in matters. Is that right, Jimmy?"

Harding said nothing. He stared at the grotesque parody of what had been his kitchen. The heart of his home. That heart had now been ripped out.

"Detective   Inspector   Veronica   Taylor.   Interview suspended." She checked her wristwatch. "8:01 P.M." She stood and picked up the document wallet, but left the six-by-eight where it was.

"Five minutes."

Chapter 5

"Cat and dog they were. Anytime you came past that lane you'd hear her screeching. Couldn't for the life of me understand why they stayed together. I suppose it was for the little one. That's what they say, isn't it?"

Macpherson poked candy out of a molar and nodded.

"You pass most evenings then?" he asked, sucking the offending gooey glob off his fingernail.

"Oh, aye. Walk Tess here thrice a day. Keeps me fit and healthy."

"So I see." Macpherson looked up at the house, feeling Reilly shoot a glare that burned into the back of head.

"Mr Reynolds?" said Reilly.

"George, please." George Reynolds was ruddy faced. A stubble resembling beard rash crowned his head, and he scratched at an impressive red beard. His belly hung below a John Deere sweatshirt, modesty just about preserved by the oversized shirt beneath. By his ankles, head cocked in observation, was a black Labrador.

"George, you didn't hear anything this afternoon, did you? See anything out of the ordinary?"

"No, Constable. I was walking back home when I saw the ambulance. Terrible. Just terrible. Julie being a nurse herself, too. She's a good neighbour. My mother had an operation, and she called in often enough to help us with the dressings. Jimmy was a quiet sort. Until he got a drink." Reynolds mimed sinking a glass. "Still, not the kind of thing you expect." He shuddered. The dog stood and shook itself.

"You ever have any bother with Jimmy?" asked Macpherson. He stroked the dog's neck and accepted the lavish attention she returned.

"Me? No. Like I said, quiet fella until he gets a drink."

"Finds his voice, does he?"

"And the rest." A low chuckle. "Look, I'll not speak ill of the wee lad. He's had it tough with work and the wee one lately, but I'll tell you this." Reynolds looked about, a surreptitious glance to confirm he was not being observed from the hedgerow.

"You'll have him on your records, you know? Previous, as they say. He battered one of the other boys in the local a few months ago. Haven't seen him in since but…"

Reilly looked at the big farmer and nodded for him to continue. Reynolds glanced towards the house.

"Nothing to say he wasn't still knocking it back indoors, is there?"

Chapter 6

"OK, run through what we know for definite," said Taylor.

Carrie Cook sat on her right. Sam Simpson remained at the recording console, laptop open. He dragged windows across onto the screens of two larger monitors, his expression not hiding his belief that they should have charged, and had Harding in the cells by now.

On the large observation screen, Henry Scott was talking. Harding was slumped over the table, leaning on his elbows, head in hands. Carrie Cook read out the summary.

"Call centre receives a triple nine call at 5:05 P.M. The caller, later identified as Harding, states there has been an accident at 179 Dunregan Road, Belfast. Confirms ambulance requirement and also police. Someone was accidentally shot."

"Do we have the recording?" asked Taylor, looking to Simpson.

"Yes," he said.

"Cue it up. I want to play it to him."

The DC nodded and set about the task.

"Carrie?"

"Armed response unit confirm no threat to life, and ambulance crew find Julie Cosgrove and Tommy Cosgrove in the kitchen. Gun shot wounds to both. Julie transferred to the ambulance and taken to Ulster Hospital. Tommy Cosgrove declared dead on scene. Shotgun secured by first responders. Licensed to James Harding. Same address. Twenty-eight years young. One conviction for driving without due care, which has expired, and a current suspended for assault. Six months ago. Bar brawl."

"Not married?"

"Kept her maiden name," said Cook. "Harding treated for shock. Didn't resist. Arresting constable confirms he was adamant it was an accident. He didn't mean it. Etcetera. Etcetera."

"Forensics?"

"Pathologist verbally confirms death as result of GSW. Diane Pearson and the scene of crime team are still at the house. Harding swabbed and clothing seized. All been sent for analysis."

"Good."

"I told you it was a hole-in-one," said Simpson.

Taylor pursed her lips and stood.

"Hold the celebrations until we confirm if it was an accident or not."

Taylor's mobile phone rang, a dull buzz from her inside jacket pocket. She let herself out of the observation room and answered.

"Doc?"

"Ronnie. Is that wastrel behaving himself?"

Taylor huffed a chuckle.

"You're not my dad. I'm a big girl. I can look after myself."

"Aye, well. Tell him if he's at his antics he'll be needing a dentist to remove my boot from his sphincter."

"Lovely image."

"What's your man like?" said Macpherson.

"Depressingly normal. I just told him the kid was dead."

"How'd he take it?"

"Calmly. He knew already."

"We had a nosey around the house. Frigging bloodbath. Short range. Twelve gauge buckshot. It's a mess."

"He's saying it was an accident."

"What do you think?"

"I think why would you be cleaning your shotgun at the kitchen table at tea-time?"

"There wasn't any sign of that, but there were a few broken cups and glasses in the kitchen bin and bits of furniture that have seen better days in the yard. Do you know what I'm saying?"

"All was not rosy in the garden."

"I've just spoken to a neighbour who says they were partial to a barney."

"Interesting." Taylor pushed off the corridor wall, nodding to a uniform constable who was passing.

"Reckons Harding has previous, too."

"Bar fight. He got twelve months suspended."

"This neighbour also says he likes a drink."

"He seems OK to me. I'll check if anyone has done a blood and alcohol."

"No bother. Anything you need from us?"

"You could touch base with the family. Break the bad news about the youngster and see if they knew of problems in the marriage?"

"Do you save all the best jobs for me on purpose?"

Taylor smiled despite the circumstances and the stark similarities that could soon exist between herself and Harding. Child dead. Wife likely to follow. Whatever crimes he would be charged with, he would face the rest of his life without a family. A victim of violence.

Her own father had died when an under-car booby trap exploded one sunny March morning. Her mother followed a year later. They couldn't put broken heart on the death certificate, but Taylor knew the truth.

"Ronnie, are you still there?"

"Yes. Sorry. Look, I'm going back in here. Let us know if you find anything I can squeeze him with."

"You sure you're OK?" said Macpherson, concern in his voice. Taylor could picture the two lines between thick bushy eyebrows and felt the warmth as her surrogate parent placed a big hand on her shoulder. Robert Macpherson had been her father's best friend and colleague. The man who stepped into the missing role and guided her through the brutal years of orphaned grief and out the other side as a well-adjusted young woman and exceptional investigator. She considered the question. Was she? Child deaths were one of the most difficult to face. Emotive and depressing. A life cut way too short. Light snuffed out before it had a chance to shine beyond the family fold. She wasn't a parent but she could empathise with the loss. She had waded through similar tragedy before.

"I'm grand, Doc."

"Aye, well. I mean what I said about Simpson. Any nonsense…"

"Goodbye," said Taylor, a grin creeping into her voice again.

"See you later."

Chapter 7

The same two familiar tones blared from the hidden speakers. Harding flinched.

"Detective Inspector Veronica Taylor. Recommencing interview. The time is 8:13 P.M. Same persons present."

Carrie Cook pointed a remote at the hi-res wall monitor and it blinked to life, revealing the Police Service of Northern Ireland Logo on a rifle green background. The bottom right corner of the screen displayed a black window and a cued media file.

"This is a recording of the emergency call placed this afternoon," said Taylor.

The black window expanded, and the graphic representation of the sound flickered along the bottom of the screen.

"*Emergency. Which service do you require?*"

"*There's been an accident.*" Jimmy Harding looked down at the table. The voice was his own.

"*Sir, do you require an ambulance?*"

"*Yes, please. There's been an accident.*"

There was a rapid series of clicks.

"*Ambulance Service. Can you tell me the number you are calling from?*"

"*I'm sorry. I'm so sorry.*"

"Sir, this is the ambulance service. Can you tell me your number and your location?"

Harding rhymed off the phone number.

"I'm at home. 179 Dunregan Road. Please, quickly. She's just...."

"It's OK, Sir. Postcode?" Harding obliged.

"What's happened?"

"Oh, my God. There's been an accident. My wife. My son. They've been shot..." There was rustling in the background. Harding was sobbing. "I'm so sorry. I'm so sorry."

"Sir, is there anyone else in the house?"

"No, it's just me."

"They've been shot?" The call handler's voice ticked up an octave. The click of a supervisory ear could be heard coming on the line.

"Yes!" Harding was losing his grip.

"Is the area safe, Sir?"

"Yes. For God's sake, they're bleeding."

"Try to stay calm, Sir. What's your name?"

"Jimmy. James Harding."

"OK Jimmy, the ambulance is on the way. Open the front door and leave it open. Have you any pets? Dogs?"

"No."

"OK. Switch on any outside lights so the ambulance crew can identify the property."

Harding could be heard moving, his breath rapid.

"OK."

"Good. Now, how many people are injured?"

"Two. My wife and son."

The call handler chipped away with more questions. Age and gender. Conscious or not. Breathing or not. Calm reassurances. They are bleeding. Where are they bleeding? How badly?

All the while, Harding's ragged breath hissed on the line.

He mumbled cries and apologies, the mouthpiece smothered by fabric. There was the distant sound of a siren, the scrunch of tyres on a pebble drive, then the audible slam of doors. Movement.

"Armed Police. Mr Harding? Mr Harding, please move away and towards the patio doors."

The click of the line went dead.

"Are you OK?" asked Taylor.

Harding was a man wearing the experience of torment in his expression. He wiped a hand over his eyes and nodded.

"Mr Harding wishes to assist, Inspector. I'd like it on the record that you had his full co-operation from the off."

"Noted. Can we have the next slide, please?"

The image Sam Simpson had on his monitor was duplicated on the interview room display.

"Image Alpha, double zero one. A Franchi Affinity Three twelve-gauge shotgun. Is that your gun?"

Harding nodded. The image on the screen was a wide angle scene photograph of the shotgun set upon the kitchen table. The image changed to close up, revealing a bloody palm print on the stock and another set of prints on the barrel.

"Jimmy, I need you to answer, if that's OK. For the recording, please," said Taylor. She could see distress in his eyes. He couldn't look at the screen. What composure he had gathered was unravelling.

"Yes."

"Licensed?"

He nodded, catching her supportive smile.

"Yes. I have a licence."

"Sporting gun, is it?"

"Clays. I don't like to…" He paused and looked down at his hands. A crescent of blood remained in the cuticle of his right thumb.

"Where do you keep it?"

"There's a gun cabinet under the stairs."

"That's the only weapon?"

"It is."

"Great, Jimmy." Taylor nodded, and the shotgun disappeared. A family photo replaced the firearm.

"Nice photograph of you all."

"Inspector, Mr Harding is traumatised and in some distress over the news of his son. Could we maybe dispense with the…" Scott jerked his chin at the picture of happier times. Taylor ignored him.

"Jimmy, I need you to go through what happened today. You've said it was an accident and I want to believe that. So, help me out. Was today a typical day?"

"How do you mean?"

"Was it same as any other Tuesday? Are you usually all home together at tea-time?"

"Depends."

"On what?"

"Julie's shift pattern."

"Julie's a nurse?"

"Cardiology."

"Not working today?"

"She hasn't been in this week." He hesitated. "She took a few days' leave. Tommy wasn't too well."

Taylor nodded, not pressing the point. It was hardly relevant now. Whatever ailment the child had, the point blank twelve bore shells had cured it permanently.

"Are you working at the minute?"

"I am. I'm a hand at the Dereks' Farm. It's up the road. We rent the cottage from him."

"OK. Someone will have let him know what happened. What is it you do?"

"This and that. I'm a mechanic by trade, so I keep the

machines up and running."

"Arable?"

"Bit of everything. He has a small herd of cattle, but the fields out our back are all rapeseed and sunflower."

"Had you finished for the day?"

"I was home for my dinner. I'd go back out from six to after eight this time of the year. There's a cut for silage and then bailing to be done."

"OK. So normal enough day then."

Harding nodded. He took a long look at the family photo, then rubbed the sleeve of his sweatshirt.

"What happened there?"

"Nothing," he said, tugging the cuff down past the angry lesions that marked his forearm and wrist.

"Looks painful."

Harding shrugged.

"Probably pulling a calf out of the hedge or trying to muck about with the hay-rake." Harding read the look. "It's a machine to flip the grass. I was replacing the spines. Sometimes they're hard to get off and you don't notice you've scratched yourself."

Taylor nodded.

"You wife ever help? With the farming stuff?"

"Julie. No, hates the countryside. She'd rather be in the city."

"I'd have thought where you were, you had the best of both worlds. Dunregan Road is what? Fifteen minutes from the city centre on a good run?"

"You can see right over the cranes to the city centre from the edge of our back field," Harding agreed.

Taylor knew the geography well enough. Dunregan Road climbed up from the A55 by-pass that looped around the outskirts of the city into the Craigantlet Hills. It passed the Victorian edifice of Campbell College and skirted the edge of the Stormont Estate, Northern Ireland's seat of power. The Portland stone of the Parliament Buildings could be glimpsed through the tree-tops as you rounded the first bend and ascended up the Craigantlet slopes. *Stoirmhonadh. The place for crossing the mountains.* An exaggeration if you were talking about the rolling hills and lush farmland, thought Taylor. Not so much if you were talking about the peaks of division and conflict that had been conquered in the grounds of the Estate one long Good Friday past.

White Cottage was on the edge of Ballymiscaw village, a collection of small businesses, farms and a tiny housing estate skimming the outskirts of Belfast city and sandwiched in the windswept wilds of the hills between Holywood on the coast and the suburb of Dundonald to the south.

"Why the move up there?" she asked.

Harding gave a momentary glance at the picture.

"A few months after we had Tommy, the job come up for me at the farm. I'd done a bit of work for old Harry with another firm and he was looking to take someone on. Offered the cottage as a sweetener. We thought it would be good for the child. The space. The animals. The Ulster Hospital is ten minutes away for Julie's work. Should have worked out."

"Should have?"

"Julie didn't like it. Too cold in the winter. She suffered from hay fever in the summer."

"I see. There are marks on your wife's arms similar to those." Taylor pointed the tip of her pen at his own arm. Harding slipped his hands under the table.

"You said on the tape it was an accident."

"It was." He bowed his head. "It was an accident."

Taylor let the lack of explanation fly.

"I need you to tell me how it happened." Taylor put down the pen and placed both palms on the table. "I know it's difficult. I know you are thinking about your wee boy. But I need to understand how, Jimmy."

"I was cleaning the gun..." he said.

Taylor picked up the pen and sat back.

"Next image, please."

The window flicked up and the screen quartered. The top two images were scene photographs. The worst of the devastation wasn't in the frame. It was easy to establish the space, though. The bottom left showed the image of the shotgun and shell casings. The remaining image was a plan view sketched out on an imaging software package. All elements were in place: storage units, breakfast table and range. Doorways offered access to the utility room, hallway and snug. It could have been knocked up in a retail chain offering zero percent finance on a new kitchen. There was one morbid addition, though. The icons dropped to represent the position of the bodies and a reverse engineered cone of ballistic spread.

"Image Alpha, double zero, two."

Harding looked at the screen.

"Do you understand what you're seeing there, Jimmy?"

Harding was mute.

"Where were you cleaning the gun?" said Taylor.

"At the table." He hesitated.

"At the dinner table?"

He nodded, mute again.

"You're no stranger to a shotgun, so at best that's reckless, don't you think?"

"It was an accident..."

Taylor leaned in.

"Jimmy, you need to tell me the truth. The absolute truth, because you aren't at the minute and I'm the only one who can help you. That image was constructed from evidence gathered in your kitchen." She pointed the pen at the screen, her eyes not leaving his.

"That gun. Your gun. It didn't discharge anywhere near the table. It discharged there. Twice. Right where the paramedics found your family."

Chapter 8

"I always think you should bring grapes or something."

"It's ICU, Sarge," said Reilly, exasperated. She stopped and turned back to where Macpherson had dawdled to read a poster.

"Aye well, she'll be glad of them if they end up feeding her through a tube for a week. If she lasts that long."

"If we had brought anything, you would have had it eaten by now. Come on. Let's get this over with."

Reilly pushed through the swing door, shoes squeaking on the polished linoleum that led to the private family area outside the entrance to the intensive care ward. Macpherson followed a few steps behind. The low voices in the room paused as the strangers entered. The conversation, like the small life a few miles away, was cut short.

"What are you doing here? You should be out making sure that mad-man is locked up for doing this to my wee girl!"

The woman didn't bother raising her voice or herself from the padding of the soft blue chairs. Her eyes were raw from crying and her face was a mask of worry and anger.

The room was small, and with the addition of the two police officers it was now uncomfortably so. The distraught woman was flanked on the seat by a younger version of herself.

"Ma. Go easy. It's not their fault," she said, giving an apologetic smile as she rubbed her mother's arm.

A man sat at her side with a few days' worth of stubble and the beady eyes and weathered features of someone used to working outside. A tall, older man stood beside a vending machine with his back to the wall. Macpherson felt a fleeting sense of recognition, as though he should know who these people were.

"I'm Detective Constable Reilly. This is DS Macpherson. You're Julie's family? Mr Cosgrove?"

"Colin." The man stepped away from the vending machine and took the offered hand.

"We're very sorry for your troubles. Have you had any news?"

"The ward sister came out twenty minutes ago and told us the doctors were working on her. That it was grave and we should prepare ourselves." Colin Cosgrove stumbled over the last words, as though speaking them aloud was tempting the faith and fate that the family were clinging to.

"What kind of animal shoots his own wee boy? His own flesh and blood. I knew this would happen. I told you letting him take her up there and away from me was a mistake. I told you!" Mrs Cosgrove broke into the wracking sobs of a broken woman, the comforting arm and words of her daughter doing little to quell the desperate grief.

"Come on, Mummy. Let's get some air. You'll call us if the nurse comes out?"

"There's a tea machine around the corner. Can I get you some?" asked Reilly.

"No, we've done nothing but drink the stuff since we came in. Thanks." The daughter helped the mother to her feet, tissues appearing from the sleeve of a cardigan. Macpherson eased to the side as they exited.

The lobby exited into a corridor and a short walk to an

automatic door that offered a sheltered breath of fresh air, if fresh could be described as stinking like a week-old ashtray. As the sensor drove the doors open, the smell wafted in.

Macpherson waited until the women were clear and the door had closed. It felt like cheating.

"Mr Cosgrove, I'm afraid we have some bad news."

"Tommy?"

"He didn't make it," said Macpherson.

The man's eyes welled up, but he blinked back the tears. He looked to the ceiling as he fought the raw emotions that emerged from the grief of losing his grandchild.

"I'm sorry. I'm sure they did all they could, but…" Macpherson drifted off. But what, but the poor craiter took the brunt of the blast and was almost blown in two? If you couldn't say anything comforting, say nothing, was his mantra in these situations.

"I expected it. I heard them when the ambulance arrived. They said they had only one adult patient coming in. God Almighty, what am I going to tell Louise?" Cosgrove wiped his eyes.

"We can do it, Sir," said Reilly. Macpherson glared at her, as he a forced a sympathetic smile at the grieving grandfather.

"We've a family liaison team for times like this. They'll be in touch before the night's out."

Cosgrove nodded. The younger man rose from his seat, where he had been watching.

"Has he been lifted? Is he saying anything?"

"You are, Sir?" asked Macpherson.

"This is Dan. Daniel Wright. He's my son-in-law. Debbie's husband." Colin Cosgrove motioned a hand towards the outside lobby.

"Mr Harding is assisting our colleagues with details about the accident," said Reilly.

"Accident?"

"We're talking to Mr Harding to get his version of what happened," said Macpherson.

Daniel Wright spat a bitter laugh.

"Good luck with that. Bastard couldn't tell the truth to save his life."

"Daniel, we don't need this…"

"What's going on?" Louise Cosgrove was at the door, cheeks as red as her eyes and wreathed in a perfume of Benson and Hedges.

"She says Jimmy told them it was an accident."

"An accident?"

"Mr Harding is in custody and we will find out how this happened."

"You better because if anything happens to Julie or our wee Tommy, I'll kill him myself."

"Louise…"

"No Colin, don't be Louise-ing me! I told you the first time she came home you should have had it out with him and not let the shit sweet-talk her into going back. He's a violent…"

"Louise…"

"Bet he hasn't told you that yet? How he beat her and she had to leave for her own safety."

"We'll put that to him, Mrs Cosgrove. The team will take allegations of domestic violence seriously," said Reilly.

"It's not an allegation, it's a fact, and it was more than the one time." She sat and then stood again.

"I made a complaint about it at the time to Chief Superintendent Law. Do you know him?" She launched the name out like a threat.

Macpherson caught Reilly stiffening at the mention of the name. William Law, chief bean-counter and pain in the arse. A man with more skill in wielding a spreadsheet than investigative process.

"I know him," said Macpherson, and gave a single nod. The woman's stare fixed on him. A sense of recognition began rising up his spine.

"Well, ask him. He'll know the history. If you had done your job the last time then my Julie wouldn't be lying in there!"

She moved away, running her hands through her hair. Macpherson worried that she might tear clumps out in rage and frustration.

He eyed the woman carefully, struggling for a minute to link the face to the name and the sense of familiarity, then it clicked. Dragged from her dinner and in obvious distress, Louise Cosgrove, former Chair of the Policing Board, wasn't dolled up to her usual polished standard. He had been witness several times to her pit-bull style in committee debate, and although she had stepped down, there was no doubt her jaws would be rag-dolling this particular case until a conviction fell from them.

"I don't know what hold he had over her, but he's a nasty wee bugger. Doesn't look it, but he is. Did you tell them about that other slut he was seeing?"

"Louise…" Colin Cosgrove was reaching out to his wife, but she batted him away.

"Connie what's-her-face." She spat the name. "Ask her what she was up to with my daughter's so-called-husband and then what he did to her when she caught them."

The bleep of electronics could be heard and the door to the ICU opened.

"What's going on here?" The ward sister stood half in and half out of her domain, identification lanyard tucked into the breast pocket of her scrubs.

"Police, Sister. We're just giving the family some news." Reilly flashed her warrant card.

"Well, do it quietly. I've seriously ill people in here." She turned her withering stare on each of them, and then, without waiting for a response, she went back inside. The door bleeped closed behind her.

Louise Cosgrove looked confused.

"What news?"

The look on her husband's face broke through her anger towards Harding, his infidelities and his attack on their daughter and conveyed more than words ever could.

"I'm sorry again about Tommy," said Macpherson.

Colin Cosgrove accepted the outstretched hand.

"Thanks, Sergeant. I don't know how Louise will cope. She doted on that wee boy."

"It's tragic, right enough." Macpherson allowed the man a second to wipe his eyes and quell the rising tide of grief that caught in his throat.

"We all did. He dug in his jacket pocket for an electronic vape and put it to his lips, exhaling a thick cloud of cherry-scented smoke.

"Family liaison will be in touch, Sir. They have your details. If you need anything, just ask them. They'll fill you in if there's anything else regarding background that we might need to know."

"Appreciate it."

The two men walked in silence through the underground car park. The rising whoop and two tones of an ambulance echoed off the bare concrete as a set of headlights illuminated ahead. Reilly gunned the Vauxhall to life. The car's exhaust fumes swirled under the glow of the overhead sodium lamps.

"Would you look at that, for God sake?" said Cosgrove.

Macpherson stopped beside him as he dropped to his haunches and examined the rear quarter panel of a white Peugeot. There was a deep scar on the paintwork and the rear brake light was shattered.

"Is this yours?" said Macpherson.

"Debbie's."

"Not what any of you need right now. Another stress."

"I just hope it's not coming in threes," said Cosgrove. "It will kill Louise if anything happens to Julie."

"She's in good hands."

Cosgrove nodded and ran a finger along the scuff marks.

"I spent last night cleaning the bloody thing. Debbie must have hit it on the way out of the drive. I'm never done telling her to park over a bit and stop reversing out."

"It'll buff up and you can swap out the light unit handy enough."

"Car mechanic in your spare time?"

"I've a daughter too. You learn to do things yourself or they'd have you bankrupt."

Cosgrove huffed a laugh, acknowledging a shared understanding. For a split second the weight of misery that was waiting a hundred yards away was forgotten.

"I'll be in touch," said Macpherson.

Cosgrove stared at the broken glass. A keen sense of its fragility and that of his daughter's precipitous situation coalesced into pinpoint focus.

Chapter 9

"How is she?"

Veronica Taylor looked across the table at the man who that morning had all the trappings of what could be classed as normality but had seen it all shattered in a single heartbeat.

She felt for him. Sam Simpson and his fraternity of close colleagues might have had a few choice names to describe her behind her back, but Taylor wasn't bereft of feeling for the suspects she chased and ran to ground. The human condition dictated that the most conservative, right-minded and right-thinking individual could snap under pressure. Yes, evil men did evil things, but the man, or woman, next door was equally capable of brutality and that was the simple truth of it. It was a sad surety that nine times out of ten the perpetrator, the killer, was known and close to the victim.

"Julie is in surgery at the minute. That's all we know. I have colleagues at the hospital and we'll be notified of any change," said Taylor.

Harding bobbed his head. The meaning was clear. If the worse comes to the worst.

"Would you like another drink, Jimmy?"

Harding shook his head, lost in his thoughts and avoiding eye contact.

"Let's just go back over this afternoon. You were home for dinner?"

"Yes."

"What did you have to eat?"

Harding looked around the table, everywhere but at Taylor.

"Was dinner ready? Was it something she had prepared or do you cook together?"

"We were having a stew again. It was left-overs from last night. I put the hob on when I came in."

"Where were Julie and Tommy while you did that?"

"Tommy was in the snug watching his cartoons. He hasn't been well, I said that. I heard the TV and looked in. He was wrapped up in his blanket with Floppy."

"Floppy?"

"It's his teddy. It never leaves his side." The magnitude of what he was saying seemed to steamroll over him and Taylor thought he might be sick. The angelic face from half a dozen photographs she had skimmed in the observation room burned behind her eyes.

"Carrie, can you fetch Mr Harding some water? Jimmy, it's OK. Take a breath. For the tape, DC Cook is leaving the room."

Carrie Cook was gone for a maximum of fifty seconds. When she returned she placed down four bottles of spring water and plastic beakers. Taylor cracked open the lid of one and poured a half measure, sliding it in front of Harding. His hand trembled as he lifted it to his lips.

"Inspector Taylor," said Scott. "May I request a break? It's evident my client is in no physical or mental condition, given the gravity of this evening's circumstances, to be pressured into admitting responsibility for something so tragic."

"I'm not pressuring him or blaming him for anything at the minute, Mr Scott. I'm trying to establish that your client's account that this was a terrible accident is true."

"You're a detective inspector, not the Health and Safety Executive," said Scott.

"And as there has been a death, it is my duty to investigate."

"If you have evidence that this was anything other than a horrible, horrible mistake then hand it over so I may review and consult with my client."

Taylor poured herself some water. She sipped it and replaced the lid of the bottle.

"I'm aware of procedure, Mr Scott. I just have a few more questions and then we can take a break. OK, Jimmy?"

Harding shrugged. From this day on, he would have no break. He was a child-killer, regardless if the charges stuck or not. That indictment would imprison him.

"That's an interesting point that Mr Scott brings up."

Harding took another shaky sip of the water. The condensation was leaving a ring on the table. He wiped it with his sleeve, the fabric pulled down to cover the marks on his arm.

"A mistake or an accident? Two different things."

"Detective Taylor…"

"You came home, put the stew on and checked, Tommy. When did Julie come into the kitchen?"

"Julie was there when I turned around. She might have been on the chair and I missed her. She was just there."

"Did she welcome you home, ask about your day?"

"No, I…"

"Did you ask her about Tommy? If he was feeling better?"

"I went to take off my overalls and wash up."

"And then?"

"I don't know. This is so hard. I can't remember. My son is dead and you won't tell me how my wife is!" Harding grabbed the sides of his head.

"When did you get the shotgun?"

"I don't know. After I got washed?"

"You were only heating the meal. Leftovers, yes? Wouldn't it make more sense to clean the gun later? When Tommy was in bed?"

"I think it was before dinner. Maybe it was after?"

Taylor shook her head.

"The stew was still in the pot. No places were set at the table."

The screen, with perfect timing, blinked up a slideshow of crime-scene shots. Cottage kitchen. Domesticity. A large Le Creuset pot on the stove. Long-handled ladle on a plate beside. Paper and crayons on the pine table. Taylor mentally checked a box on Sam Simpson. Alert and on the ball. Perhaps he could be moulded after all.

"Did you argue?"

Harding dropped his hands to the table, fists bunched, eyes screwed shut. The muscles of his jaw clenched tight.

"How would you describe your relationship, Mr Harding? Loving? Volatile?"

"I loved my wife," said Harding.

"Loved?"

"I love my wife," he said, drawing out each syllable.

"Are you a violent man, Jimmy?"

"No."

"Never?"

"Are you going to bring up Freddie Moore now?"

Taylor opened the manila file tucked under her left elbow.

"Frederick William Moore. Twenty-five. Victim of a sustained and serious assault. Broken nose and jaw. Hairline fractures to the skull. Treated for severe concussion. If it hadn't been broken up…" Taylor left the obvious potential hanging between them.

"It was…"

"Don't say an accident, Jimmy," she said.

Harding glared. For the first time, there was hostility towards her in his expression.

"What was the fight about? Banter gone bad? Spilled drink?"

"He was upsetting Julie."

"Oh, I see. Very chivalrous."

"He was accusing me of things. Calling her names."

"What was he accusing you of?"

"He was drunk. Chatting a load of rubbish. I told him to back off, and he came at me. I was defending myself," Harding protested.

Taylor slid a copy of a hospital report and accompanying photograph of the injuries to Freddie Moore.

"That's a big step over the line of defence, Jimmy."

Harding looked at the broken, bruised and bloody face.

"What was he accusing you of?"

"He told Julie I was sleeping with his sister."

Chapter 10

"Is this the place?"

Reilly pulled into one of the small car parks that bookended the Bucks Head. The public house was set back twenty feet from the main road that cut across the hills. A few benches were placed under a Guinness harp and an awning which had both seen better days. A cigarette bin adjacent had a grin of ash stamped on its face, and a carriage lamp illuminated the front doors. From inside warm light and dull conversation spilled out.

"Bit out of the way, but I've been in worse," said Macpherson, clicking off his seatbelt and reaching for the door handle.

Reilly blipped the locks and followed, side-stepping a pothole and acknowledging the nod from a smoker sheltered in the lee of the old farm building's gable wall.

"Ah, I can see why the booting didn't put him off." Macpherson held the door as Erin followed him inside.

They both unzipped their jackets as they entered the public bar. Logs sparked in an open grate, a pile of hand-cut turf was stacked on the hearth and the smell of polish, beer and food service was heady in the air. The porch had opened directly into a seating area, with half a dozen round tables enjoying a brisk trade. The left and right sides mirrored each other: small open snug, raised banquet seating and dim lights. The bar itself was on the left-hand side. Polished oak and a long brass foot-rest. Optics gleamed and pumps offered a selection of local and popular transatlantic fare.

"Oh, smell that? I'm starving." Macpherson rubbed his belly as he negotiated a couple tucking into two juicy steaks and sharing a platter of thickly cut chips.

"Do you ever give your jaws a rest, Sarge?"

"That's why you've no man in your life yet, Erin. You haven't worked out that the way to our heart is through our stomach."

"What can I get you?" The bar steward was in his fifties, with close-cropped sandy hair and a genial smile. He carried the broad shoulders of a man who had spent his days in manual labour and was either making a few quid on the side or had decided he'd given enough to the fields and was closing time in less strenuous toils.

"Freddie Moore?" Macpherson held up his warrant card. The bar-man turned up his lower lip.

"Not yet, Officer." He glanced at the clock on the wall to his right. "Regular as clock-work, mind you. Give it twenty minutes?" A wary look. "Has he done a mischief?"

Macpherson shook his head and offered his hand.

"No. Just a few questions he might help with. Do you know him well?" The barman's hand dwarfed even Macpherson's massive mitt.

"Bobby. Pleased to meet you. I know him as well as any of the regulars." He cast a vague look to the end of the bar and the snugs where drinkers supped and swapped the spoils of the day's gossip.

"Pint of Tennent's then gets a Vodka chaser when the shutters are coming down. Usually takes the lasagne if he's eating. Works the quarry over by the crossroads. He's a bit

43

boisterous but not a bad lad. Is this over the beating?" Bobby frowned as though an unpleasant smell had wafted in.

"It might be. You here that night?"

"I was. Pulled that bloody nutter off him. I heard the police were up at the cottage. Has he been at it again?"

Macpherson tutted. "Can't really get into it." The barman nodded, accepting the brush off.

"Drink?"

"Aye, go on. We'll wait. Erin?"

"I'll have an orange juice, please." Reilly scanned the crowd, spotting two seats tucked in an alcove by the front porch. Macpherson nodded his understanding as he caught her eye.

"I'll bring them over. I'll have the same, please. And a couple of packets of bacon fries."

"I'll get you a menu, if you want?"

Reilly, now seated at the table rearranging beer mats, overheard and raised her chin. Macpherson humphed.

"Crisps will do."

"It's on the house. I'll bring it over," said Bobby.

"Here, keep the change. Appreciate it but you wouldn't believe the antics of anti-corruption these days." Macpherson put a ten pound note on the bar and collected the crisps, threading his way to Reilly.

"Excuse me?"

Macpherson paused his step and met the outstretched hand of a small balding man. The arms of his navy overalls were tied around his waist and he was wearing a check Tattersall shirt and brown wool tie.

"Can I help you, Sir?"

"I'm Harry Derek."

Macpherson nodded as realisation dawned.

"Mr Derek. DS Macpherson." He offered the man a refill.

"No thanks. A half is the limit for me, Sergeant. May I join you a minute?"

Macpherson ushered Derek to the table and introduced Reilly. On his heels, a waitress delivered the drinks and excused herself.

"Terrible business." Derek looked like he meant it. Macpherson nodded in agreement.

"There's quite a bit to get through but chances are you'll have the cottage back by this time tomorrow, Sir," said Reilly. Derek waved a hand.

"No rush. Take the time you need. If it's true, I can't believe it."

Macpherson took a sip of his orange but said nothing.

"We can't discuss it, Sir," said Reilly. "But, if there was anything different about Mr Harding's temperament, state of mind or general demeanour of late it might help us piece together a picture. You sure you won't take a tea or something?"

"Have you tasted Bobby's tea? There's better to be found in the roadside shuck." Derek smiled, but it pained him. Events at the cottage and the outcome for the young family seemed to be weighing on him.

"Jimmy's a quiet wee lad. A very diligent worker. Never late. Doesn't skive. I just can't believe it of him."

"How long has he worked for you?"

"Good three years now, although I know him this long time."

"Generally, he's no trouble?"

"If I'd another couple like him, I'd be a happy man."

"Reliable?"

"Oh aye," Derek nodded. "The odd day here and there. Plays a bit of rugby. Has had a few black eyes and the odd knock but it has never stopped him coming to his work."

Macpherson gave a sharp nod. Qualities he admired. It aggrieved him how many of the new generation of coppers seemed to swerve a day and take advantage of the generous sick package available. Reilly braced for his 'In My Day' speech, but it never came. Instead, "Nothing seemed on his mind?"

"He was a bit distracted today. Took off early. He'd cleared up his work, though."

"Did he give a reason?"

"I never asked. I'd an idea something was bothering him. Christ, if I knew it would lead to this…"

"He didn't say what the something was?" asked Reilly.

"I think it was more someone."

Macpherson nodded in understanding, jerking his head towards the bar.

"You heard me asking about Freddie Moore."

Harry Derek's eyes narrowed. He clicked his tongue. "I did. That's part of the reason I wanted to speak with you."

"Oh? Sounds ominous," said Macpherson.

"I had to let Freddie go from the farm. It wasn't long after Jimmy came on. I'll be frank in saying there's some animosity between the two."

"I'd say that's an understatement by the medical records."

Derek spread his palms.

"I agree that in black and white it looks bad."

Macpherson, unable to resist any longer, snapped open the bacon fries, offering the packet around. To his delight, neither Derek nor Reilly accepted. He plunged in, popping three in his mouth, and crunched.

"Jimmy's lucky he didn't go down for it," he said, around a mouthful of the reconstituted corn snack. He dipped his fingers in for seconds.

"Freddie thinks Jimmy had something to do with me dismissing him, but that's not the case. He was a liability. Nothing grand. There was no one incident and I gave him the benefit of the doubt, but the fella just wasn't a worker."

"Do you think Freddie started on Jimmy Harding that night?"

"I was here. I know that's how it was. He was shooting his mouth off about him stealing his job. I gave him short shrift and told him to pack it in. Then he got personal." Derek blushed.

"Jimmy told him enough was enough, but Fred wasn't having it."

"The eyewitness reports say Jimmy had to be pulled off him?"

The old farmer gave a resigned shrug.

"That he did."

"What did he say that riled Jimmy so badly?" asked Reilly.

"He told him stealing his job was bad enough, but he wasn't having him knocking off his wee sister into the bargain?"

The two detectives shared a look.

"His sister?"

"Connie Moore. Freddie told the entire bar, including Julie, that Jim and Connie were having it away. Jimmy went mad after that."

"This was months ago. What's going on now?"

"Freddie's been hassling Julie again. In the shop. On that social media." He gestured to Reilly's phone. "Telling her they're still at it and there's isn't a damn thing Jimmy can do to stop him or he'll find himself banged up."

Chapter 11

"Is that what you argued about?"

"We weren't arguing."

"Jimmy, something happened this afternoon that has resulted in us meeting like this. You've told me it was an accident but I don't believe you," said Taylor.

"What you believe isn't relevant, Inspector. You have a burden of proof to establish and if you don't start presenting your case, I'll be advising my client to reserve his right to silence." Henry Scott sniffed and rearranged himself, smoothing a Hugo Boss marine blue and rouge silk tie.

Fair enough, thought Taylor. She could appreciate that Scott was playing his cards as they fell. He wasn't the most pugnacious brief she'd ever faced, although obviously adept given the high end clothes and the hundred and fifty quid Parker pen he was scratching notes with.

Julie Cosgrove was in surgery, little Tommy was dead, and in the absence of any other living witnesses she was going to have to crack Harding. It looked bad for him. He could call one discharge accidental. But what was that but gilding the lily of recklessness? Or gross negligence. Two discharges were nothing short of deliberate.

Scott knew one very simple key point. One that Taylor was acutely aware of. The clock was ticking.

"How long have you been married, Jimmy?"

"Six years."

"Generally speaking a happy one?"

"I already told you I love my wife."

"It isn't a trick question."

"I suppose it's happy. We've had our ups and downs," he said.

"Who doesn't? Moving jobs, house, raising a child. They all add degrees of pressure."

"Are you married, Inspector?"

It wasn't a question she normally faced from suspects, and was one that wasn't touted out too often. Those in her limited social circle knew her marital status, and those who moved through the periphery of her life that didn't were colleagues, both legal and enforcement, usually asking another question in a roundabout way.

Taylor was single. Not through lack of suitors, but she made a stand not to date within the job and didn't have the patience to put up with the sly looks and innuendo that would slip in when her profession came up with those outside.

She was committed to her work, dedicated to following in her father's footsteps and exceeding the expectations she imposed upon herself. It required tunnel vision and a lack of distraction, and she guarded her spare time fiercely. When she thought about it, she would accept that watching her mother's grief and subsequent decline following the death of her father had had a detrimental effect, skewing her view on the social norm of pairing up, having children and seeking the happy ever after. The experiences of ten years in the job also highlighted reasons that put paid to the reality of that fairytale.

"I'm not," said Taylor.

"We loved each other, but we fought from time to time.

Stupid stuff."

"Like who was supposed to take the bins out?"

"Yeah. Like that." Harding's expression softened. A memory from the past.

"Did you have much of a social life together? I know it must have been difficult lately if Tommy had been ill, but you had family to lean on, right?"

Harding's wistful expression darkened.

"My folks are dead."

Taylor felt a sharp stab under her ribs. The spark of a kindred spirit.

"I'm sorry, Jimmy." A mental flash of a little body in the morgue blinked once in her mind's eye. "Times like this you need your parents."

Harding shook his head. He sniffed and scratched his nose with the back of the hand.

"God, I hate to say this. I sound like a broken record." He looked at Taylor. "It was an accident. They were on a caravan holiday in Scotland. Head on with a lorry. It was a while ago, but it never really leaves you."

Taylor regarded the sorrow in his eyes. She felt the pain of having loved ones snatched away.

"I know."

The hum of the air-con and the click of the thermostat were the only sounds in the room for several moments.

"What about Julie's family?"

Harding puffed out his cheeks.

"We didn't get on. They didn't like Julie coming out to the country."

"Really?"

"Yeah. You'd think we were moving across the world, but they're so tight knit. Her parents, aunts, sister. They all lived practically next door to each other. Latch-key. I hated it. Someone would always just walk in and it would be a job to get them to leave."

"You felt you'd no privacy in your own home?"

"Something like that. They didn't understand what the problem was. Her mother went mental when we moved up to the cottage."

"Not regular visitors?"

"No, Julie would run down into the town with Tommy for a visit, but it was rare they came to us."

"Did you never join them?"

"I wasn't all that welcome. I'd do Christmas Day. That was about it."

"OK."

"Look, there's something else."

"Uh-huh?" Taylor was scribbling in her notes.

"You'll find out soon enough. I'm surprised Louise hasn't been on to you already, baying for the noose to be brought back."

Taylor sat back. He'd tell her in his own time. Head shaking, he leaned forward suddenly, stabbing a finger on the table.

"I loved my wife. OK? But they're going to tell you all the problems we had and how she ran back home. That's true. She did for a little while, and she took Tommy. But we worked through it. We sorted it and she came back of her own free will."

"OK, Jimmy. Sounds normal to me. Couples fight, need a bit of space."

"They said I beat her. I didn't. I swear I never laid a hand on her. Fuck, it was an accident. I walked out of the barn with a plank to fix up Tommy's playhouse and hit her on the nose." He threw back his head, sighed and splayed his arms wide.

"We laughed about it, for God's sake and then we had some stupid fight and she ran home. Next thing Louise is on the phone threatening all sorts. She has connections. You know? To the police. She made complaints at the time."

Cook thumbed the tablet on her lap, dabbing passwords to databases.

"When was this?"

"A while ago."

"A month? A year?"

"Not quite a year."

"Not quite a year," said Taylor. "About the same time Freddie Moore told Julie you had been sleeping with his sister?"

"I wasn't shagging his bloody sister!" Harding jumped to his feet, then his anger deflated like a burst balloon. He looked around as though lost.

"I wasn't. I loved my wife." A tear bloomed and broke free.

There it was again, thought Taylor. Loved. Past tense.

Chapter 12

Another drink each and a further packet of crispy treats for Macpherson, and true to form Freddie Moore made his regular appearance through the doors of the Bucks Head. It was more of a stumble than a grandstand entrance, but as regular as they'd been assured, nonetheless.

They recognised him straight away.

In the intervening time since they had bid Harry Derek a good evening, Reilly had scoped Freddie Moore out on his social media. Why he believed hiding behind an avatar and running out a diatribe of abuse against Jimmy Harding, the Dereks and Julie Cosgrove for the crime of remaining with her husband, offered any form of anonymity or excuse was beyond her. They had both watched dumb-founded as his audacity intensified, posting videos of verbal abuse from the window of his car or in the supermarket aisles. Others showed him doing a drive-by of the Hardings' cottage and setting off fireworks over the roof of the house.

"See, Harding knocked no sense into him," said Macpherson, then rose from his chair as Moore walked past.

"Freddie Moore?"

"If this is about the hedge clippers, I took them back. Jesus, have you people nothing better to do?"

Moore was a good foot taller than either detective, but Macpherson doubted he weighed half as much as the diminutive Reilly. Whatever Derek had employed him for, his obvious talents had been overlooked. Jam a bucket hat on the fella's head and you could stake him out in a field to scare the birds.

"We don't know anything about hedge clippers, Mr Moore," said Reilly, brandishing her warrant card and a disarming smile.

"You're cops though?" He glanced over Reilly's shoulder. He was stranded between the door and the bar.

"Aye, son. We are. Hoped you might have five minutes."

"What about?"

Macpherson tilted his head towards the vacant table. From the corner of his eye he noticed Derek pulling on a gilet and searching his pockets for the means to settle his bill.

"Jimmy Harding."

A gleam appeared in Moore's eyes, along with a self-assured smugness.

"Oh, aye? What about him?"

"Can we sit?

Moore shoved his hands in the pockets of his coat and considered it, accepting the offer after a beat and following Macpherson's outstretched hand.

"Drink?"

"Pint of Tennent's," said Moore, unbuttoning his khaki military-style jacket.

Reilly gave the order at the bar and re-joined them, setting the lager in front of Moore, who grunted a thanks.

"Who's he give a kicking to this time?"

"What makes you think that?"

"Because he's a psycho." Moore set down his pint and tilted his head to the right. He parted the hair above his left ear. "See that? That's what Jimmy Harding is capable of.

Nutter."

A jagged line of old stitch marks scored an angry welt across his skull.

"What happened that night, then?"

"This happened." Moore pointed at his own head. Macpherson nodded to him to continue.

"I told him to stay the fuck away from my sister."

"Connie, right?" said Macpherson, receiving a grunt of acknowledgement. "How did you know there was something between them? Did she confide in you? Did you catch them on?"

"I didn't need to catch them on. I've eyes in my head, don't I?"

"To be clear, you saw Jimmy Harding and your sister in a compromising situation?" said Reilly.

Moore pulled a face as he downed a draught of his lager.

"Christ, no!"

"So how did you know?"

"Jimmy was never away from the shop. She works in the Spar, the garage. Down the road?"

Reilly nodded at her sergeant. They had passed the Maxol signage and the small forecourt that fronted the convenience store, off-licence and chip shop on the way up the hill to the Bucks Head.

"Aye, well. Every night she's on, he's hanging about. Fawning over her. Buying her a bar of chocolate. Having a wee coffee. Laughing his bloody balls off at me." Moore stabbed a finger into his chest. His face was darkening as he played it all back in his mind.

"Maybe they were friends?"

"She's twenty-one, and he's a grown man with a wife and child. What would she see in him?"

"Age is just a number," said Macpherson, seeing where this was heading.

"He's a bloody predator is what he is. I told him to back off one-too-many times. He didn't, so I told his wife what he was up too and he done this. Scarred me for life. Could have killed me." Moore pointed to his head again.

"It stopped after that?"

"He was heart scared he'd get in any more bother, so yeah. Until lately and he's back pushing the boundaries."

"Which is why you are hassling him again?" asked Macpherson.

Moore's expression turned stony.

"Hassling him? You're saying that like he's the bloody victim."

"What my colleague is saying, Mr Moore, is given the history between the pair of you, why are you still content to pressure Julie Cosgrove about her husband's alleged relationship with your sister?"

"You don't think she should know her man's running around after a wee girl half his age? She should fucking ditch him and take the child. That would sicken his happiness."

"And this has nothing at all to do with you getting the bump from the Derek farm and Jimmy taking your place?"

Moore choked as he swallowed a sip of the Tennent's. His eyes watered as he cleared his throat.

"Is that what the sly wee bastard's told you?" he said.

"Mr Moore, harassing a member of the public at home or in the shops and posting it on-line could be viewed as breach of the communications act. If you don't knock this vendetta on the head, it will be you who ends up in the courts."

"I'm doing a bloody service making sure everybody knows that sicko is preying on wee girls."

"Your sister's a grown woman, son."

Moore set down the remains of the pint. Lager was sloshing from lip to lip like an angry amber ocean.

"I'm done here."

He pushed off from the table and the glass fell. Reilly snatched for it, but it was too late. It spilled. She righted the glass. Picking up a dry napkin, she wiped her fingers then dropped it to soak up the worst of the mess.

"Julie Cosgrove could've had you done for harassment. So could Jimmy, for that matter. Have you any idea what might have happened if one of those rockets had hit the house?" she said.

"Piss off." Moore was unapologetic for the mess and unrepentant for his actions.

"Where were you at half five today?" said Macpherson.

"What?"

Macpherson shrugged. "Where were you at half five?"

"Why? What's happened?" Moore was suspicious. His eyes darted to the door, then to the lager dripping off the table.

"I didn't say anything happened."

"Christ, has somebody took a pop at Jimmy?" He looked down at the upturned faces of the two detectives.

"Were you anywhere near White Cottage at half five?" asked Reilly. She could see the cogs starting to freewheel. Panic? Hope?

"I didn't do anything."

"You sure about that?" Macpherson, aware of Reilly's look, dropped the wind up.

"Did you see anything?"

Moore may have towered over the detective, but the steely look and the air of authority radiating off the smaller man made him feel as tiny as a field mouse. He also knew at that point that something had happened. And he wished more than anything that he could answer in the affirmative and have been there to see it.

"I was at the quarry. You can check with my foreman. We had a problem with one of the conveyors and I ended up getting away late."

"You weren't stalking Jimmy or his missus, then?"

Moore for once looked shame-faced.

"No. No, I wasn't near them."

Macpherson pushed back his seat and stood. His hope for an eyewitness pooled around his feet like the dribbling remnants of Moore's lager.

Chapter 13

Jimmy Harding paced the room and then, as realisation dawned that his nightmare would have to continue for some time yet, flopped onto the seat and put his head in his hands. He stared at the floor.

Carrie Cook dabbed the tablet on her lap as Taylor watched the observation screen. Her attention wavered as Henry Scott scowled on the monitor that showed the landing lobby. He had paced in parade square for the last few minutes with his phone clamped to his ear. The pained gestures and slump of his shoulders suggested he was trying to explain why he was still stuck in a custody suite and not home enjoying a TV dinner or a restaurant date. The phone disappeared inside the tailored wool-blend jacket, and his expression wasn't dissimilar to the one Macpherson had when Diane Pearson was explaining the trigonometry and quadratic equations of a ballistics report or Professor Thompson was extolling the different physiological impacts of smothering, choking, strangulation and asphyxia.

"Does someone want to help Mr Scott with his coffee?" she said.

Sam Simpson glanced up at the screen.

"I'll go." He jumped up, then paused when he reached the door.

"Erm, would either of you like one?"

Taylor looked to Cook, who had started. Her eyebrows arched.

"I'll have a tea please, Sam. Black. No sugar," Cook said.

"Guv?"

"I'm fine, thanks," said Taylor. An amused smile curved around the corners of her mouth as the door closed.

"You must be a positive influence, Carrie."

"I'd say your reputation precedes you, Guv."

"It hadn't an hour or so ago." Taylor turned. "I'm not that bad. Am I?"

Cook tucked a lock of hair behind her ear and re-crossed her legs.

"Have you not heard the stories Doc tells us?"

Taylor chuckled.

"Half aren't as interesting as he makes out and the other half aren't anywhere near the truth."

"It's the way you tell them," said Cook. Her tablet beeped, and she dabbed the screen.

A Detective Constable for two years, Cook had been seconded to Taylor's team for what should have been a brief period of support during an investigation into a domestic slavery ring. She had fitted in like she'd always been there and shown both an ability to get the job done and an inherent aptitude for investigation. She was also an excellent communicator and a dream to put out in the field to deal with witnesses and family liaison in what had been a sensitive case. Taylor had petitioned to keep her, and it delighted everyone when the transfer was approved. Especially Macpherson, who she indulged with Tupperware boxes full of home-baked cake and savouries.

"Hospital update, Guv."

"Good or bad?"

"Julie Cosgrove is out of surgery. Next twenty-four hours

are crucial but prognosis is better than it was three hours ago."

Taylor nodded. Jimmy Harding could have been freeze-framed. He hadn't moved position since she last looked. Only the slight rise and fall of his shoulders confirmed he was breathing.

"You going to tell him?" said Cook.

"Yes. I think he deserves to know. At the very least it might focus his mind on the fact that there's going to be another version of events than just his."

"Maybe not for a while though."

Taylor nodded.

"Do you think it was an accident?" Cook asked.

Taylor had been thinking the same thing. She could nail down guilt straight off the bat normally. A combination of gut and psychology. Unconscious tells, deliberate untruths and hours locked in small rooms with bad people.

Harding sat somewhere in the middle of the Venn diagram. She wouldn't say he was bad to the bone. He was guilty. She could feel it coming off him in waves. But guilty of what? Was it infidelity? Spousal abuse? The unbearable grief of killing his own son?

The chirps of the access code being entered pulled her from the thoughts of pity that even though Julie Cosgrove would survive, Harding would nevertheless find himself alone.

"One tea. Black no sugar and two Kit-Kats." Sam gave a trademark smile as he put them on the table.

"Figured you could use the sugar hit," he added to Taylor, his earlier frostiness thawing.

"Thanks, Sam."

"I miss anything?"

Harding had shifted position and looked down the barrel of the camera. A man facing his executioners.

"Julie Cosgrove will probably pull through," said Cook.

"Good. Well, isn't it?" He noted Taylor's expression.

"Would I want to wake up and find my only wee boy was dead instead of me?" Taylor shrugged.

The atmosphere in the room cooled. Cook sipped her tea and Sam booted the laptop back up.

"Carrie, give the hospital a nudge and request an opinion on the injuries to Julie Cosgrove's wrist and chest. I want to know the probability they were defence wounds."

"Guv."

"And chase up Diane Pearson. SOCO will have their hands full at the scene, but anything they have that puts Jimmy Harding on the trigger of that gun I need to know ASAP."

Cook nodded, moving her tablet and phone to the small alcove behind the door. Her tea was balanced on top of her notebook.

"Sam."

Simpson's fingers rattled across the keyboard as he launched internal network and browsers. He looked up expectantly for Taylor's instruction.

"Let's see what else we can dig up on Julie Cosgrove. If her mother used her connections they'll be recorded. Any previous callouts to the cottage or any previous addresses. Reports of domestic violence, withdrawn statements. Hospital visits. Jimmy Harding is hiding something and I need to know what it is so I can hang him with it."

Chapter 14

Reilly swung the tail of the Vauxhall into a parking space and clicked on the handbrake. There were half a dozen pumps in the forecourt that fronted the Spar convenience store, and she had found a bay in the thirty or so that skirted the small shopping complex. A workman in orange coveralls collected cash from an ATM a few bays down. He glanced in their direction, tucking his wallet back in his pocket as he entered the store. Traffic zipped by on the main road, headlights sweeping over the Maxol sign displaying fuel prices and an offer on meal-deals. Macpherson had perked up at that as they drove in.

The first waft that hit Reilly as they exited the Vauxhall was the warm, enticing embrace of fried potatoes and battered fish. A smell from childhood. Seasides and smiles, car journeys, amusement arcades and the bracing wind of the north coast.

"...fish supper. Portion of chips. Two battered sausage and a curry sauce?" The door to the chip shop was ajar, and the voices of the counter staff drifted out on the tide of heady scents. Reilly watched as a server handed across a weighty paper bag to a female customer. Office clothes, hair scrapped back and seeking an easy fix for dinner. The woman smiled wearily as she exited to find Macpherson standing in the path. She skirted around him, juggling the bag under one arm and fussing in her handbag for car keys with her free hand.

"No," said Reilly. "I can see what you're thinking. Let's get this over with. I swear I don't know where you put it. You must have worms or something."

Macpherson stood in front of the large glass window like a child peering longingly at a Christmas display.

"I've worked through my dinner break, Missy. You can shout me chips when we come out for being so insubordinate."

"Insubordinate?"

"Aye. Here's me teaching you the benefit of a lifetime's wisdom and you, barely out of the training college, have the front to be telling me I've an eating disorder."

"Come on. You're not getting chips. You'll stink the car out."

"You're getting as bad as bloody Ronnie. Do you hear me?" said Macpherson, quickening his pace to catch up to the young DC, who had already disappeared inside the store.

The shop was relatively busy. Commuters between Belfast and the outlying towns of the North Down coast were stopping to grab ingredients for their tea or a few snacks and other confectioneries for a night in front of the television. Reilly approached a young man knelt stacking a fridge full of yogurts and brightly labelled milkshakes.

"Excuse me? Hi, can I have a word with the manager?"

The young man had to focus a second as he looked up at her, adjusting his thick glasses.

"Is there a problem?"

"No, son. We just need a word with the boss." Macpherson stretched out a meaty mitt with his warrant card on display. "Police."

"Oh, right. This about the drive-offs? Come on up to the

tills. I'll page her."

Nathan, as his badge identified him, stood and beckoned them to follow. They negotiated a few dangerously driven trollies and a queue of customers elbow to elbow at the reduced-price shelf before he ushered them into a small space beside greetings cards and a rack of magazines. Macpherson plucked one out and began thumbing through.

"You seen this?" He waved a picture of a celebrity luxuriating on the white sands of a Balearic beach.

"Would you put that back?"

"I mean, what the hell was she thinking? She was a pretty wee lassie before she done that to herself. There should be a law against it."

"It's the in thing."

"She looks like a bloody duck," said Macpherson, incredulous that a syringe full of collagen might achieve anything resembling enhancement.

"It's harmless."

"Oh. Thinking about it, are you? I can picture you." He puckered his lips into a pout.

"God help your wife, Doc," said Reilly. Macpherson flapped the magazine closed and replaced it on the shelf.

"I swear I'm waiting on our Moira telling me she's going for some. She never has that lot off the TV."

Reilly chuckled. She shook her head, considering whether a drop of Botox or fillers might in any way be more damaging than being Macpherson's long-suffering spouse.

"Hi. Thanks for coming. Nathan said you're here about the drive-offs?"

The young woman who had appeared from the double door behind the till was bright-eyed. She wore her blonde hair up in a mop on the top of her head and was fresh-faced with an attractive smile. Her green fleece, company logo resplendent on the breast, was easily two sizes too large and made her head look too small for her body. Macpherson clocked her name badge.

"Connie Moore?"

"Yes. I'm the assistant manager. I called it in," she said. Straight white teeth. Bright green eyes. Flawless skin. Reilly saw why Jimmy Harding would be attracted. She was beautiful without trying.

"Miss Moore, we aren't here about the drive-offs."

She raised manicured brows, caught on the hop.

"Oh."

"Is there an office where we could talk? Somewhere private?" said Reilly. The line of customers were trying not to look at the two police officers and the petite assistant manageress.

"God, it's not Freddie, is it? What's he done?"

"If we could just…" prompted Reilly.

"Yes, of course." A roll of the eyes. A been-here-before look. "Come through."

Connie Moore thumbed a mechanical code-lock and led the two detectives along a short corridor. Trollies of goods to be stocked were on one side, with bundled stacks of discarded packaging ready to be recycled on the other. She paused at the last door on the right, which was wedged open. The room beyond smelled of burned toast.

"Can I get you tea or something?"

"I'm fine, thanks," said Reilly, picking the one seat which didn't have crumbs or stains on it. Macpherson looked around.

"Was anyone killed?"

Connie laughed. It was a sing-song lilt, and again Reilly could see what Harding might have seen in the girl.

"In the explosion? I know. They're no better than children, honestly. Look at this!" Connie plucked a polite notice to clean as you go from the waste bin.

"Tea? Coffee?"

"I'll give it a miss, thanks," said Macpherson, looking at the sink full of muddied cups, stained tea-spoons and soiled cutlery. Connie dragged a seat across the floor and stood up to reach a large plastic container.

"Clean. For visitors." She settled the box on the worktop, clipped off the top and produced two clean white mugs.

"Aye, go on will. Coffee. Black. No sugar. Oh, none for me," said Macpherson as Connie fished out a packet of shortbread and plated a few. He caught Reilly's arched brow.

"She's only after saying I need to lose weight."

"She did not?" said Connie.

"Aye. She did."

"You're in fine form. Don't be letting anyone tell you different." Connie laughed as she passed across a cup of instant coffee. Macpherson blew across the surface and took a sip.

"You sure?" she said. Reilly nodded.

"So, what can I help you with?"

Macpherson tilted a red seat and tipped the crumbs and a foil biscuit wrapper to the floor. He repositioned the seat before sitting down.

"It's about Jimmy Harding."

Connie gulped down the mouthful of tea. Her eyes flew wide.

"Freddie hasn't…"

"No. Your brother hasn't done anything untoward," said Macpherson.

"Has he hurt himself?" Connie asked. Each word wavered with an edge of emotion.

"No. No, Jimmy Harding is fine."

"Thank God." She sat, not bothering to check the state of the chair. She clamped her hands around the warmth of her mug.

"Can I ask the nature of your relationship with Mr Harding?" said Reilly.

Connie's face twisted in a scowl that still didn't touch her soft prettiness.

"Don't tell me? My brother has sold you some story along the lines of I'm being groomed by Jimmy Harding. Well, I'm not. We're friends. That's all."

"How did you meet?" said Reilly.

"I met him at the farm. Harry Derek introduced us. I did casual work there when I was finishing my A-Levels. We got to talking. I met Julie through Jim. Did some child-minding the odd weekend. Not that there was much to it. Tommy was always asleep. Didn't peep. It let the two of them get out to the pub for a couple of hours."

"Did Jimmy ever make a pass at you?" said Macpherson.

"Christ, no!"

"We've had a few people mention that your relationship maybe stretched beyond platonic?"

"Why? Because we got on? Had a laugh? Just because a fella and girl enjoy each other's company doesn't mean they're rolling around together," Connie said, her face flustered.

"There was nothing more to it?"

Connie took a sip of tea, wary eyes on each detective.

"Should there be?"

Macpherson watched her put the cup to her lips. He was hopeful she would never feel the need to cosmetically augment the fine Cupid's bow. He looked to Reilly, who was watching the girl with rapt attention too.

"When Jimmy put your brother in hospital, did it not sway you off him?"

"Freddie deserved it." She looked at Reilly as she answered. "Almost every sinner in the bar at the time comes in here. I got the full account. Freddie never could let me make my own decisions."

"Still. A bit extreme?"

"Jimmy is... was under a lot of pressure."

"We spoke to Harry Derek. He didn't strike us as the sort of boss you couldn't talk to if you were having problems," said Macpherson.

"It wasn't work. Sorry, I thought this had all been sorted. Jimmy had his day in court and is on a suspended. If you're looking for someone to put the boot in and get him a custodial upgrade you're talking to the wrong person."

"Did you ever speak to Julie Cosgrove about Jimmy?"

"I tried." Connie's lips tightened, and she gave a brief shake of her head.

Macpherson let her have another drink. He took a sip of his own coffee and considered how much he was about to tell her.

"Mr Harding was arrested earlier today."

"What?"

"I'm afraid so. We've seen the social media stuff your brother has posted. Was it causing animosity between Jimmy and Julie again?"

"Again?"

"She left him for a time after the assault."

"She was never happy he turned to me instead of her." Connie stood. She sloshed her tea into the sink and dumped the cup on top of the others, then leaned against the worktop with her arms crossed.

"Turned to you about what, Connie? The court case? Julie leaving him?"

"No," she tutted. "Jimmy was depressed. He was hurting himself."

Macpherson blinked. He hadn't expected that. Reilly flipped a page in her notebook.

"Hurting himself how?"

Connie shrugged.

"Cuts. Burns. I caught him in the outhouse at the back of White Cottage. He'd been drinking. I saw him put a cigarette out on his arm." She tapped a spot below the line of her shoulder.

"Why?" said Macpherson.

"He was just down. His own folks are dead, you know? Julie's ones wouldn't give him the time of day."

"Did you ever meet the Cosgroves?" asked Macpherson.

"No. I saw Julie's mummy on the TV. She was something to do with the police?"

Macpherson nodded.

"Jimmy said she wasn't one bit happy when the two of them got back together. I think she might have been pushing behind the scenes."

"Pushing for what?"

"Julie was giving him a hard time over moving back to the town. She could be a real hard case. Always on his back about something. It was hard to watch sometimes. Jimmy said she was wild for the first six months they moved up here."

"Wild how?"

"She had went through a bad time. Post-natal. It sort of dragged on. Jimmy said there were days you couldn't look at her."

"That's quite an intimate thing to be sharing," said Reilly.

"I suppose, but he needed someone to talk to. I never judged him. I like to think it helped. I offered to break the ice with Julie about it but..."

Macpherson saw deep empathy in the young girl's eyes. Whatever feelings she had for Harding, whether genuine friendship or a misplaced crush, he had no doubt they were heartfelt and well intentioned.

"Are you a trained counsellor, Connie?"

"Me?" She laughed again. "No. Jesus, I work in a Spar

shop."

"Julie Cosgrove is in hospital. Jimmy shot her."

Connie's hand went to her mouth.

"No, he wouldn't. He couldn't."

"You see why we need the unvarnished truth about your relationship?"

"Oh my God. Poor Tommy. "

Macpherson caught Reilly's stare. Flip you for it. He paused a beat.

"I'm sorry, but little Tommy was hurt too," he said.

Connie stared blankly, not comprehending what Macpherson was skirting around.

"Tommy died, Connie."

"No."

"I'm sorry..."

"No!" she roared, backing away from them. Tears bloomed and her face was caught in an ugly grief-stricken rictus.

"He wouldn't. He loves that wee boy. There's no way."

"When did you last see Jimmy Harding?"

"He wouldn't."

"Connie?" Reilly moved towards the woman. She seemed to have shrunk further into the oversized fleece jacket.

"Connie? When did you last talk to Jimmy?"

"Earlier. He was here after lunch." Connie was on the brink of hyperventilating. Reilly sat her down and squatted beside her, placing a comforting hand on her back.

"How was he? Did he say anything?"

"He asked to see me after work. Wanted to talk."

"What about, Connie? Did he say why?"

The tears flowed unbridled. Her words were distorted by sobs.

"What was that?"

"She told him she was leaving for good and taking Tommy with her."

Chapter 15

"So we are explicitly clear. You are aware this isn't the first time?"

Chief Superintendent William Law twirled a pen in his fingers for want of having a moustache to play with, but the effect remained eerily reminiscent of a Bond villain ready to cut loose the rope and deposit someone to the sharks.

Bunkered behind his roll-top walnut desk, he refused to blink until Taylor had the temerity to furnish a reply.

"DC Simpson has just pulled the records," she said.

"And?" Law had removed the spectacles over which he would normally fix his gaze, and had placed them on an A4 pad of scribbled notes. His left ear was red and his immaculately groomed hair was ruffled. The mobile phone responsible was face down beside the glasses.

"I've gleaned the basics, Sir. I was about to take a deeper dive when you requested to see me."

"This Harding. He's guilty? Yes?"

"He doesn't deny it."

"Good. Get on with charging him then. You're aware who the victim's mother is?"

"Yes, Sir."

"I know the woman personally, and while she no longer holds a position on the Policing Board, she has enough clout with the Executive and in the press pool to throw this under a very bright spotlight. I don't agree with trial by headline, Veronica, but if Harding is admitting to this, it's in our best interest to charge him and get him off our hands. Am I clear?"

"Crystal."

"Keep me appraised. You're dismissed."

Taylor nodded her understanding and stood. Law had already replaced his spectacles and was returning to strategise on how to keep his own and the service's reputation intact by stage managing the coming storm whilst spinning the facts of how a domestic abuser, with a history of violence, had been free to murder his child and almost succeed in killing his wife.

"She's positive about that?"

"As far as believing what Harding was saying was true, yes," said Macpherson.

"What did you make of her?" Taylor put out her foot to hold open the door for a passing uniform and brief making their way up from the custody suite. She smiled in recognition as the solicitor gave a jaunty wave and mouthed a greeting. She shifted the phone to her other ear as Macpherson answered.

"Nice kid. The wee girl is fond of him. She's adamant he doesn't have it in him. Was in bits about the child, too."

"Where is she now?"

"We dropped her home. They called in a manager to cover. She was in no state to work, and she's shocked to be at the centre of something like this. I told her we would send someone to the house for a full statement."

"I'll get Carrie to ask Sergeant Harris to get one of the section crews over," said Taylor.

"How's she doing?"

"Grand. Slick is proving useful too. Believe it or not."

Macpherson answered with a grunt.

"Doc, if Harding was on the limit and she was about to walk out with the kid, he could well have snapped."

"Aye. It's possible. It also clouds the water if his brief goes down the line of diminished responsibility by way of mental illness."

"I'll have Simpson pull his medical records to see if he is under treatment."

"Connie Moore told us he had struggled since his parents died. Julie Cosgrove also suffered post-natal depression and I think he found that hard to deal with too."

"I guess the in-laws didn't help."

"Aye. I met them in the hospital."

"I've just been in with the Chief Super. Mrs Cosgrove has been through her Filofax and he's getting his ear bent by those on high," said Taylor.

"Did you ever meet her?"

"No. She'd stepped down by the time I came along. You?"

"Saw her in action a few times. Rottweiler, but she was straight enough," said Macpherson.

It was a distraction that Taylor didn't need, and one that might easily derail impartiality in a heartbeat. Especially if the person rattling the sabre was known as a straight shooter. Great strides had been made to remedy incest and nepotism within the halls of criminal justice, but fear and favour could still be brought to bear. Particularly with something as emotive as a child's death and a desperately ill mother.

"Where are you now?" she said.

"Heading back to White Cottage. We'll have a look for any medication in Harding's name and take a snoop around the outhouses. If he was hiding out there to booze and self-harm, we might find something to hit him with before the doctors come through on your end."

Taylor took the final few steps to the landing of the

interview suite and drew a deep breath as she keyed the code-lock to the observation room. It was better than doing nothing.

"OK. Let me know if you find anything."

Chapter 16

Taylor clicked the door closed behind her and looked at the big screen.

Harding looked as though he'd been in the chair for forty hours instead of four. Henry Scott was also beginning to lose his own polished veneer. His jacket hung over the back of the chair and his neck-tie was loosened an inch. Client and brief were in a one-way conversation driven by Scott. His questions were answered with a simple nod or half shake of Harding's head.

"Guv." Carrie Cook stood, sliding her tablet across so Taylor could view it. "Preliminary forensic reports from the doctor. Jimmy Harding's blood alcohol is negative."

Hadn't been drinking then. Taylor mentally checked the box. "Any other drugs?"

Cook paused. She cocked her head to one side and flicked back a few screens, then winced apologetically.

"We didn't ask for a specific screen. Do you want me to get it run again?"

"No. I do need you to request access to Harding's medical history, though."

"Specifics?"

"Treatment for depression. Stress. Doc has a statement saying he was suffering badly and may have been self-harming to cope."

"Jesus."

"Yeah. I know. We need to find out if he had ever presented for treatment or had a diagnosis for psychosis or similar behavioural traits," said Taylor.

Cook nodded. She dabbed the tablet to bring up a new window.

"Doctor McCall's office emailed over the death certificate for Tommy Cosgrove." She paused. There was a moment of silent reflection as the grim document loaded up.

"Professor Thompson also sent his initial brief from the scene. Death consistent with gun-shot wounds from close range. This backs up his previous verbal, and he has scheduled in the autopsy for first thing tomorrow. Usual time."

Taylor nodded. Just another indignity on the family and for little Tommy Cosgrove to endure. Cook briskly moved on.

"Diane Pearson's report. She told me to tell you to take this section with a pinch of salt until she has it corroborated at the lab." Cook had highlighted a selection of paragraphs.

Di Pearson was the Forensic Science Service senior crime scene investigator and the site team lead. Taylor had a long and trusted relationship with her and she knew Pearson well enough on a professional level to understand that her comments were a humble attempt to downplay her near psychic skill in the deciphering and analysis of the evidential patterns she picked up at the scene. Cook drew up a picture of the shotgun lying on the terracotta tiled floor. Two little yellow evidence markers were positioned uncannily like a McDonald's arch.

"She's sure the palm prints here and here will be Harding. Compare them to the size of this one here, which is smaller and more likely to belong to Julie."

"She tried to grab the gun?"

"That's what it looks like. There are fingerprints on and around the trigger guard, but she's warning they may be too smudged for use."

"OK. Anything else?"

"The lab has returned analysis from the clothes we seized. Blood from both Julie and Tommy Cosgrove and a significant quantity of gun shot residue. Probability is high enough to put Harding behind the trigger. They need to carry out some more tests but it's looking good."

"Good work. Get onto the doctor's report before we go back in."

"Sure thing."

"Sam." Taylor smoothed her hair back. Law's insistence that she get this one over with was niggling at her as the thought of sitting through little Tommy's autopsy haunted the back of her mind. "What have we got?"

"You were bang on with the mother." Simpson launched a new window and dragged up what he had uncovered, listing it chronologically.

"No incidents at the couple's previous address but Mrs Cosgrove placed fifteen calls through switchboard, reporting her concerns, within the first two months of the move to White Cottage. It was followed up on the first half dozen occasions, but Julie Cosgrove told them her mother was overreacting and she was fine. The officers attending were granted access to the dwelling and reported no signs of disturbance."

"Get those reports anyway and find out who it was. Have Sergeant Harris pull them in if need be. I want to run it through with them face to face."

"Yep. No problem."

"Is that when she escalated things?"

"Yes. She cornered the Chief Inspector's secretary at a Policing Board lunch and got an audience. His office pushed it back down to Inspector Kinning, and he got the same dead end."

"It's hard to know whether it was maternal concern or just plain nuisance," said Taylor.

"Sounds like she was sticking her nose in. Any wonder Harding didn't get on with her."

Taylor watched over Simpson's shoulder as he pulled up a copy of Julie Cosgrove's medical history.

"The mother provided this, but again Julie Cosgrove denied anything untoward and made no complaint."

Taylor looked at the diary entries of attendances to medical services, then a second batch of reports recording injuries sustained by Julie Cosgrove over a period of months. They began with the move to White Cottage and continued up to a week before Jimmy Harding was arrested for the assault on Freddie Moore. The visits started innocently enough.

An investigation into bouts of severe asthma and migraine. A diagnosis of stress related to the move and coping with a young child in an unfamiliar environment. A prescription for back pain and a torn anterior deltoid. They became more overt from there. X-rays for a broken arm, which turned out to be a severe strain, and treatment for cuts and abrasions. Julie Cosgrove put the injuries down to domestic mishaps or horseplay in the grounds of the cottage.

At the bottom was the referral report from social services, who had attended on a number of occasions and reported that Julie Cosgrove, Tommy and Jimmy Harding were managing well and met the threshold to sign off with no further action being required.

Someone's dropped a bloody bollock here, thought Taylor, as she scanned the dates and plotted the escalation of the injuries alongside the course of Freddie Moore's vendetta against the family.

As she made to speak, one comment caught her eye. The

description of a wrist injury. Running to a paragraph, it detailed the patient presenting and passing it off as a gardening accident. The physician had noted the treatment plan, but what was perhaps more incendiary, had commented that the welts and damage to the dermis and significant bruising to the wrist and forearm were consistent with defence wounding. Taylor took Simpson's mouse and clicked on the jpeg file attached. She took a step back to better take in the picture. She'd seen those marks before, on Harding's arm a short time earlier, and on the photographs of Julie Cosgrove sent across from the hospital.

Harding's insistence that the day's events had been a horrible accident was now looking more unlikely than it ever had.

Chapter 17

Reilly took the proffered clipboard and scrawled her name, then passed it over for Macpherson to do likewise.

"Thanks," she said, handing the scene log back to the constable on the gate of White Cottage.

"You can pull up over there," he said, indicating a spot beside one of the SOCO vehicles. "If you park on the verge, you'll get side-swiped, the speed they come around that corner."

"You should set up a speed camera, son. Earn yourself a wee bonus," said Macpherson. The constable pulled a face.

"That's likely right enough, Sarge." He pointed to a spot beyond view further down the winding road. "The inspector had us on one down the hill this afternoon. Where the national meets the thirty? Wish I was on a commission, I can tell you that."

"The bean-counters always like to see a lift in revenue this time of the month. Somebody has to pay to have me ferried about in this luxury." Macpherson offered a wink and tapped the roof of the car through the open window.

Reilly thanked the young constable again and negotiated the cattle grid, pulling up in the turning circle outside White Cottage beside an overgrown pedestrian gate. It was the same spot she had parked at earlier. All the lights were still on.

"Do you need me to get out the crow bar?" she said, opening the door and already halfway out. The headlight warning tone pinged.

"You need to learn to respect your elders," grumbled Macpherson.

Reilly popped the boot. She slid across the trunk of Tyvek oversuits, booties and gloves.

"What are you doing back? Are you looking for tips on how to do proper police work?"

Diane Pearson shaded her eyes from the headlights. She pulled her face-covering off, allowing it to hang over one ear as she dropped her hood and shook out a bob of ash blonde hair.

"You must have a big holiday booked, Di. You're fair eating through the overtime budget today," said Macpherson, fighting to shake out his overalls.

Pearson laughed.

"How do you stick him?" she asked. Reilly shrugged.

"He's not that bad as long as you keep feeding him."

Pearson chuckled and zipped the front of her suit to her navel. She huffed a breath.

"What's the craic with you right enough? Something come up?"

"We had some unconfirmed on the suspect's medical history. We were going to snoop the bathroom cabinet. That sort of thing."

"Well, we're practically finished up. Not much more we'll glean that isn't already on its way back to the lab."

Macpherson paused in his battle with the polyethylene oversuit.

"Does that mean I can skip this rigmarole?"

"Are you going anywhere near the primary crime scene?"

He shook his head, giving a nod to the upper windows and

then across the wildflower meadow.

"Bedrooms, bathrooms, and over in the outbuildings. Did your lot have a look in there?"

"Yes and no. We scouted the house, but there's nothing to suggest anywhere other than the kitchen is the primary. Booties and gloves, and if anything is out of place, you tell me straight away. Gun cabinet under stairs is OOB."

"Did you notice much booze about the kitchen?"

"You having that sort of day?" said Pearson. Macpherson chuckled, rolling up his crime scene suit.

"No. From memory no wine rack. Fridge had one tin of Guinness," she said.

Macpherson nodded, satisfied with the answer. He tossed the suit at his DC.

"Thanks Diane," said Reilly, catching Macpherson's balled up overall and lifting out the box of blue overshoes and nitrile gloves.

"Try to keep him out of trouble."

Reilly acknowledged she would, and Pearson searched in her pocket for keys and blipped open the forensic vehicle. She took a seat and a sip from a bottle of cola stowed in the door bin. She waved as the detectives moved off.

Reilly handed Macpherson his gloves and booties on the front steps of the cottage. A dream-catcher hung in the window next to a pair of small wellington boots, and a child's anorak was hooked by the hood on a brass hanger screwed to the side of a larger coat stand.

"Let's see if the boffins missed anything then," said Macpherson, leading the way.

The porch opened into a large, brightly lit reception hallway, with up-lighters and a large glass chandelier in full flame. The stairs to the first floor were on the right, with the entrance to a family living room and the kitchen on the left. A WPC masked, gloved and shod in overshoes stood sentry as they entered. Macpherson confirmed that they had signed the scene log and explained that they would be doing a search of the first floor. The WPC waved them on. Voices and the sounds of Pearson's team packing up equipment in the kitchen drifted through. There was a short peal of laughter as they went about their work.

Macpherson let Reilly take the lead up the staircase. The carpet looked newly laid, the pile angled from the brush of a handheld vacuum.

The landing was wide. Clean. Decorated in soft colours and furnishings. A radiator cover held a vase and pictures of the family. The master bedroom was at the end, with two other rooms between it and the top of the stairs. One was decorated in bright blues and greens, with dinosaurs on the walls and picture books on the floor. The other was a dressing room. It had floor-to-ceiling wardrobes, a dressing table and a set of drawers. The main bath was next to it.

"You check in there. I'll nosey in the master," said Reilly.

It didn't take long to find what they were after.

"Nothing in the bathroom," said Macpherson.

"Found these." Reilly held up several small packets of medication, the label of a local pharmacy on the front stating dosage and a warning.

"Sertraline. In Jimmy's name. Full packet, but the issue date was a fortnight ago."

"If he was off his meds and it's true she'd dropped the bombshell she was leaving, it adds to the hypothesis that he snapped."

Reilly dropped the packet and the pills into a clear ziplock evidence bag.

"Right. Outhouse then?"

Chapter 18

Reilly collected a torch from the boot-kit of the Vauxhall and they walked in file across the luxuriant grasses from the gravelled turning circle to the two-storey building in a similar whitewash to the cottage. An automatic floodlight illuminated an arc out to thirty feet. The mammoth shadows of the moths and daddy-long-legs fluttering around the heat danced across the field. The long stems of meadow cats-tails lashed at their legs and the rainbow heads of larkspur, blanket flower and English marigold which were a sea of swaying colour in the daylight, were dark in their wake.

"Age before beauty," said Reilly, unlatching the old door and nudging it open with her toe.

Macpherson took the offered torch and stepped across the threshold.

He cast the beam around the door frame and thumbed an old bakelite switch. The dull click-clonk of fluorescent overheads warming up echoed in the dark, and then there was a low hum as they flickered to life and illuminated the space.

Aside from the single door through which they had entered, there was a set of doubles, lashed closed with a chain and padlock. A decrepit Nissan under a dust sheet nosed against the doors. Its hubs were rusted and it was up on a trolley jack.

The rest of the main floor comprised a lawnmower, a couple of ride-a-long cars, a rocking horse with the name Ruby hanging from its straggly mane, a few push-bikes with flat tyres and stacks of wooden packing crates. Stairs led up to an old hayloft, with several of the planks that formed the steps and at least three spindles missing.

Along the rear wall was a counter-top with cupboards above and below that once had been an old kitchen but had been retrofitted to form a workshop. Oily engine parts, the flywheel from a strimmer and a selection of tools scattered the surface or were hung on nails tapped into a wooden backboard. Shapes were stencilled around with a thick-tipped marker.

The whole place smelled of damp, cut grass and fuel.

"Over there," said Reilly, indicating a spot cleared in the far corner with a small table, a work-lamp and an armchair that looked older than herself.

"That's quite the collection," she said as Macpherson eased up beside her.

A large wicker basket held the remains of at least thirty bottles of spirits. Reilly picked out a few branded vodkas and gins, but most of the others had names she didn't recognise and labels screaming out budget paint-stripper. Beside the work lamp was an ashtray of crushed butts and a double-edged Wilkinson Sword razor blade.

"That's a serious stash to get through," said Macpherson, his knees cracking as he squatted to lift out a bottle. He held it to the light to better read the back.

A piece of bright material was wedged down the seat cushion. Reilly pulled it out. The centre was stained and crusted with what could only be dried blood.

"Bag that," said Macpherson.

Reilly did as directed. Macpherson reached down to pull

an old trunk from a space under the bench.

"Erin?"

"What is it?"

"Get Diane."

Reilly peered over his shoulder. In a bed of rags was a broken wine bottle. The serrated edges were black, and her guess as to what it could be was confirmed as Macpherson played the light of the torch along the bottle to where the slim neck was strangled by five bloody fingerprints.

Chapter 19

Henry Scott's words shrivelled on his lips as Taylor entered Interview Room 3. Her expression carried a storm of impatience and her face was set in stone. Carrie Cook followed. She eased the door closed. The engagement of the lock seemed much louder in the tense atmosphere.

"Interview continues 11:47 P.M. Same persons present." Taylor set down her notebook and placed her phone and pen on top of it.

"Jimmy, I'm tired. You look shattered, so cards on the table. I'm not pissing around anymore. What happened at White Cottage this afternoon?"

"Inspector, can I object? Your tone is..."

"Mr Scott. You're not in court now so why don't you keep your objections for someone who's willing to listen to them?"

Cook felt a flutter of anxiety in the pit of her stomach at the confrontation. She jammed her pen between her teeth to suppress the need to grin, a ridiculous side effect she had borne since childhood that had done her no favours at home or in class.

"Jimmy. Good news. Julie has come through her surgery. She will, with a bit of grace, be fit for interview once the medical team gives us the OK. So, this whole fabricated story of an accident is going to get an entirely new perspective once the sun comes up."

Harding paled and brightened all at once.

"She's OK?" He put his hands on the table and leaned in, eyes wide.

"No. She's not OK," snapped Taylor. "She's had life-saving surgery for a gun-shot wound that rightfully should have killed her." Harding took his hands away, ghostly palm prints evaporating.

"And then when she does come round, someone is going to have to tell her that her dear wee boy is dead!"

Harding opened his mouth to speak.

"Shut up, Jimmy," said Taylor. A glare at Scott was enough for him to heed.

"You've been lying to me all day, and to be frank I'm a bit pissed off."

"I didn't..." Harding crossed his arms, resting his big hands on his own shoulders. His cuffs rode up.

"You didn't what? Shoot them?"

"No..."

"You didn't shoot them now?"

"It was an accident."

"Was beating Julie an accident too?" said Taylor. "Sam."

The wall monitor blinked to life. The PSNI logo disappeared, to be replaced by a vivid jpeg image in glorious gory high definition.

"Image Bravo, zero one. Looks nasty. Do you want to state what it shows?" Harding lowered his head.

"Julie Cosgrove. Moderate bruising to the face and subconjunctival haemorrhage to the eye. I've got the doctor's notes. Walked into a cupboard door."

Taylor looked across the table. Harding was staring at his hands, now folded in his lap. Scott looked to the screen, noting the injuries and date stamp.

"Next," said Taylor. The image changed. "Two weeks later.

Patient returned presenting sudden onset of pain to upper left arm. Lost footing. Treated for muscle strain and received X-ray to right hand. Significant internal bruising to proximal phalanx of thumb and metacarpal. Painkillers prescribed. You don't have to write all this down, Mr Scott. We'll be here a while. I'll have DC Cook prepare you the reports afterwards. Do you remember what's next, Jimmy?"

Harding mumbled. He shook his head. When he looked up there were tears in his eyes.

"A bit louder please."

"A cracked rib," he said, defeated.

"Three. Cracked. Ribs," said Taylor. "What happened this time?"

"She slipped on the stairs."

"She slipped on the stairs. Have you any idea how pathetic that sounds? She fell twice? Inside a week? There's more incidents after these. Can you remember them all?"

Harding opened his mouth to speak, then closed it. He looked to the ceiling and wiped his tears. Taylor tapped the file under her hands.

"This is just a case of systematic spousal abuse. Was it the drinking, Jimmy? Did it get out of hand? Arguments ended up getting physical? You weren't drinking today, so we won't be using that as an excuse to mitigate what you've done."

"It was an accident," Harding shouted. The silence after the abrupt outburst was deafening.

"It must be the most accident-prone house in bloody Belfast," said Taylor.

Bzzzt. Bzzzt. Buzzt.

Taylor's silenced mobile hummed. The dull resonance was amplified by the desk. She picked it up and glanced at the screen. Macpherson. The call cut off before she could silence it.

"I was almost sympathetic to you earlier," she said.

"You've lost your son. Your wife is hanging on by a thread. Now…" She pointed at the livid red ridges on Julie Cosgrove's torso. The deformity of the cracked bones was visible below the skin, stark against the white cotton of her bra.

"Now it looks like you're a man with an anger problem. One you took out on Freddie Moore. One you take out regularly on your wife. What happened today? Why did you turn that gun on your family?"

The hiss of static preceded the flat tone of the room-to-room intercom.

"DI Taylor. Can you break a moment?"

Taylor looked into the camera and nodded. She collected her phone, her pen and the folder. Cook followed suit.

"I wonder what else we have." Taylor stood, looking down at the now pitiful shell of Harding. His eyes were raw. He was unable to look her in the face.

Scott ran a finger around his collar. He at least, understood the weight of the growing evidence against his client and how it could tip the scales when it came before a jury.

"I suggest you two have a final brief. When I come back in here I expect it to be with the final nail, and after that I'll be recommending the PPS throw everything including the kitchen sink at you."

Harding placed his hands on the table, a foot apart, ready for the shackles. His chin was on his chest. The inevitable conclusion had been reached.

"Interview suspended. 12:08 A.M."

Chapter 20

Macpherson leaned back against the formica work-top. He glanced to his left to make sure he wasn't about to bang his head on the old kitchen units.

"Are you sure? Do you not need more light in here or something?"

"I'm sure," Pearson nodded. "I'm going to have them sent for testing, but I'm telling you, ninety-five percent. These are Julie Cosgrove's prints. I've lifted enough in the kitchen to tell the difference. Look." She held an index finger up to the fan of prints around the neck of the broken bottle. "Similar. She has delicate wee hands like me."

"But you're sure?"

"Pretty sure." Pearson arched a brow. "I can't be a hundred percent until we do a proper match against the control sample, but I'm as sure as I can be standing here. Do you want the rest of these dusted?" A sudden scowl clouded her face as she calculated the number of stashed bottles.

"Won't do any harm," said Macpherson.

"What about the edge? Is it blood?" asked Reilly.

Pearson half nodded.

"I'd say it's likely. We'll run it too."

"Thanks, Diane. Sorry," said Macpherson. "It's been a long day. I didn't expect to drop more on you."

"I'll get the crew over. We'll have these done in an hour or so."

"Keep me in the loop, won't you?"

"No worries. Tell your boss I'll have reports on the kitchen out by tomorrow afternoon."

The two detectives expressed their gratitude and left the outhouse as Pearson called her team from the van where they had packed up and were waiting to leave. Two gloomy faces passed them in the wildflower meadow.

"All about the OT lads," said Macpherson.

"Not much use to me tonight. I had a table booked with the missus at eight."

"Just think about all the ways the double time can buy her affections back."

"It'll be six weeks before I see it, and I'll be hearing about the job being more important than her the whole time."

Macpherson chuckled as the grumbles turned to distant mumbles. Pearson's business voice greeted them as the men entered the pool of light spilling from the outhouse door.

"Is that us then?" said Reilly.

"I think so. I'll just give Ronnie a call and give her the…" He cut short, thumbing the end button on the call. Reilly's head appeared from behind the boot lid.

"What is it?"

Macpherson pulled a fresh glove from his pocket and knelt down. The gravel scrunched under his weight. He twisted and put a hand on the column of the pedestrian gate wrapped in luxuriant green hedgerow.

"Torch?" he said. Reilly passed it across. He clicked the beam on and swept it across the ground beside the rear wheel of the Vauxhall.

"Shit, did I hit the…" Reilly lowered the boot lid. She stopped, her hand running over the intact rear lamps of the car. The ground under the rear wheel sparkled with shards of toughened coloured glass. Macpherson played the beam up the gate post to a broad white streak of paint.

"The SOCOs are going to frigging string us up," said Reilly as Macpherson stood to face her.

Chapter 21

"What is it, Sam?"

"Harding's GP reports just came through," said Simpson.

"And?"

"Your wish is my command." Simpson pushed his chair across to the conference table where he had already spread the paperwork out.

"Now these all coincide with the timeline we have for Julie's injuries. You'll see that up to this date," Simpson double tapped a letterhead with a fingernail, "there are several sports injuries and one incident he reported as an accident at work." Simpson turned in his seat and clicked his mouse.

"That injury should have been reported to the Health and Safety Executive. He was off for over three days. Harding, or rather his boss, Harry Derek, didn't follow it through."

"He probably didn't want the inconvenience of having the place shut down. It shouldn't but it happens all the time. What was the injury?"

"They thought it was a broken wrist, but it was a severe sprain. He was put in a splint and on pain relief, which stopped him operating machinery."

"I'll get Doc to speak with Derek in the morning. What else have we got?"

"He had two bouts of concussion and a visit for eighteen stitches. Football injury. Elbow to the face." Simpson mimed jumping for a header.

"I think he played rugby," said Cook.

"It was rugby," said Taylor.

"Anything consistent with his wife fighting off a beating?"

"He had ointment prescribed for deep scratches to his arms and shins. The GP report backs up his own statement that it was in the course of his work."

Taylor nodded, skimming ahead. Then she slowly ran her eye back across the documentation.

"When did the anti-depressants start?"

Cook helped scan the paperwork, with Simpson giving a few clicks of the keyboard and mouse.

"Eight months ago," they replied in unison.

"Give or take around the time he took up with Connie Moore."

"Maybe she did get him to seek help."

Taylor sucked her teeth.

"What's this one?"

"Glazing the outhouse. Slipped on the ladder. Twenty-five stitches to meat of his right forearm," said Simpson. He scooted back to the table and looked at the page Taylor was reading.

"These two need locking up in a padded room where they can't hurt themselves," he said. Taylor shook her head in disbelief as she read another entry.

"We have two adults here. Parents. Regularly seeking treatment for injuries sustained at home and they have a young child. Are there any independent reports from the health visitor or passed on to social services from the GP? The last one I read had given them the OK," said Taylor.

"No," said Simpson, distracted as the laptop pinged a tone.

Taylor picked up a psychiatric evaluation from Harding's

GP. He was under pressure at home and at work. He'd been sleepless, restless and agitated. Was he stressed? Most likely. Depressed? Probably. Had he thought about injuring himself? Sometimes. Had he thought about doing worse? Not seriously. He wished he could just stop the world, but he wouldn't leave his boy fatherless.

"Here's the report from Sergeant Harris. The incidents when uniform attended." The DC shifted his seat so Taylor and Cook could look over his shoulder at the monitor.

Taylor read down the mail. The calls had been placed by Julie Cosgrove. When Echo One Two had attended the scene, her husband was profuse with apologies for wasting their time. Julie Cosgrove likewise.

She could read the frustration between the lines in the report. Domestic incident. Evidence of alcohol. Both parties apportioning blame to themselves. Matter resolved.

"Nothing on things looking out of hand?" asked Taylor.

"That's it. Heat of the moment. Sorry, officer. Won't happen again," said Simpson. Taylor turned away just as the laptop dinged again.

"Oh. Hold your horses."

"The sarge has added an amendment. He spoke to both PCs after he'd pulled the report. Meadows from section four said she remembered the two incidents she attended. It wasn't the first time. She'd been called out to have a word in the past over violent conduct. Says it was quite a few years ago, but she was certain she recognised the householder, although it was with a different spouse."

"She'd been out to Jimmy Harding for a previous domestic years ago? Why do we not have that on his file?"

Simpson clicked the attachments. He blew out a slow whistle as they downloaded.

"Get everything we can on this. Now." Taylor dropped Harding's psychiatric evaluation on to the table and pulled out her phone.

Chapter 22

Reilly had guided the Vauxhall down the winding bends of Craigantlet into the suburbs of the sleeping city. The midnight glow cast a dome over the valley from the rich farmland on one side to the desolate Black Mountain and the bleak silhouette of Cavehill across Belfast Lough. A Norwegian gas tanker was making steady progress in the thread of black water that lay between blinking anti-collision lights.

The A55 was dead, which was to be expected until the rush hour kicked in after seven o'clock the next morning. The Sydenham by-pass was the same. The neon fronting of George Best City Airport was still ablaze, but the last flight had landed hours earlier to beat the noise curfew and the first commuter flight to the UK wasn't due to lift off until after six. A single taxi was parked in the lay-by below the airport footbridge, the driver catching a doze behind the wheel.

The carriageways turned into arterial suburban roads lined with shuttered shops and the occasional flare of a takeaway that was still open.

Reilly pulled into a cul-de-sac of narrow, manicured hedgerows. The pavement was tree-lined, the terrace houses dark. The single sentinel of a streetlight cast a pool about halfway down. On the turning circle at the end, four larger semi-detached properties stood equidistant from each other, bordered by low redbrick walls and wrought-iron railings. Light seeped between a crack in the curtains of number twenty-three.

"Still awake then," said Macpherson.

Reilly ratcheted the handbrake and killed the ignition. The engine block ticked as it cooled.

"You sure about this?" she said.

"We're here now…"

The front door of the house opened and Colin Cosgrove exited, barefoot and wearing pyjama bottoms and a grey hoody. He was carrying a stack of pizza boxes and an empty milk carton. As he dumped them in the recycling bin, his head jerked up, startled at the noise of the car door opening.

"Jesus. You scared me there."

"Guilty conscience?" said Macpherson, a disarming smile as he approached.

"Has something happened?"

"Colin? Have you left the door open?" Louise Cosgrove's voice drifted from the hallway. The porch carriage light blinked on and illuminated a small front garden with perennials in bloom. A Toyota Avensis was nosed into the narrow drive and a Peugeot was reversed into a smaller paved spot under the front eaves

"Mind if we come in?" said Macpherson.

"Daddy?" Debbie Wright appeared in the light, her face rosy from a scrub. Her hair was piled on top of her head and the fleece collar of her dressing gown was pulled up.

"Is it Julie?"

"Can we come in?"

"Yes. I suppose. We aren't long back from the hospital." Cosgrove offered them entry. Debbie turned and headed for the kitchen, calling her mother.

Macpherson walked into the broadside as he passed the

bottom of the stairs and waited for Cosgrove to close the front door.

"What do you want?" Louise Cosgrove was similarly dressed to her daughter, wrapped in a long peach robe. She had a glass of wine in hand. "Has something happened to Julie?"

"Lou, give them a minute. Through there, Sergeant," said Cosgrove, gesturing to the front room. A television flickered in the bay window. A news channel was dissecting the day's headlines from Westminster and around the world. Cosgrove muted the volume and sat on an armchair. The Belfast Telegraph was folded in the seat's seam and two remote controls were lined up on the arm. He picked up a mug from the floor and took a sip of tea.

"Have a seat."

"Never mind a seat. What's going on?" said Louise.

Reilly took a perch on the edge of the three-seater nearest the television and furthest from the door, where Louise Cosgrove brandished an angry glare. Macpherson stood at parade ease. He edged the vertical blinds aside and peered into the drive.

"Your wee car, Debbie?"

"The Peugeot. Yes. Why?"

"Was with your dad when he spotted a nick out of it," said Macpherson, letting the blind fall closed.

"Is this about the bloody tail-light?" said Colin Cosgrove, swallowing another sip of tea. His elbow caught the remote and knocked it to the floor.

"It is," said Macpherson.

"Sergeant, if you've come to my house in the middle of the night to tell me you've found who crashed into Debbie's car…" Cosgrove groaned as he bent to retrieve the control.

"Is that it? You're rapping my door for that when you haven't put that animal Harding behind bars yet? The bastard that took our wee boy and you're worried about a stupid hit and run?" Louise Cosgrove's voice rose, the hand with the glass wavering. "Get out of my house and don't come back unless it's to tell us you've charged that piece of filth. I've a mind to ring Chief Superintendent Law now and tell him where his subordinates' priorities lie."

"Debbie, were you up at White Cottage today?" said Macpherson.

"Me? No." Debbie shook her head.

"You didn't see Julie at all today?"

"I was working."

"All day?"

"Yes."

"Why are you questioning my daughter?" Louise Cosgrove commanded the centre of the lounge.

"Debbie, tell them nothing. What is this, Sergeant?" She set the glass of wine on the mantelpiece and put her hands on her hips. "How dare you come in here at this time of night with this carry on?"

"Mrs Cosgrove, I'm sorry. I understand this is the worst of times, but I've questions I need answered."

"You do. Like, why was he allowed to walk the streets and kill my grandson?"

"When was the last time you spoke to Julie?" Macpherson turned back to Debbie. She shifted, her hands in her dressing gown pockets.

"Two days ago."

"She came for lunch," said Louise. "We had a bit of a catch up. He was making her miserable again. Back running after that tart."

"She wasn't happy," Debbie agreed. She sat on the opposite end of the couch to Reilly. "We told her to just leave him."

"And was she going to?"

"She said she'd think about it. She had Tommy to think of."

"Where did that get either of them? He didn't deserve that wee boy. I hope he bloody rots." Louise snatched up her wine and sank it.

"I think she was going to this time. I do. I really do," said Debbie.

"Are you done? Can this car thing wait until another time?" Colin Cosgrove stood and placed an arm around his wife.

"Not really," said Macpherson.

"For God's sake, I don't need to claim on the insurance or want to press charges. Whoever hit it, let them alone. Concentrate on putting Jimmy Harding away."

"Did Julie take a drink?"

Louise Cosgrove sucked in a breath. Her husband broke in before the fury.

"What's that got to do with anything?"

"Might be something. Might be nothing."

"Get out," Louise snarled. Macpherson let the tension wash over him. Debbie stared at her slippers.

"Debbie?" said Reilly.

"She…"

"Out!" Louise Cosgrove hurled her glass across the room to shatter above Reilly's head.

"Jesus. What's all the bloody noise?" A bleary Daniel Wright entered, wearing a washed out tee and shorts and rubbing his eyes.

"What's going on?" He looked from face to face.

"Nothing. They're going," said Colin Cosgrove.

Reilly stood, flicking shards from her hair and a few large pieces of glass from her jacket.

"I'm afraid we can't," said Macpherson. "Debbie, why were you at your sister's this afternoon? You reversed the car into the gate. There's paint on the post and glass on the drive.

The forensic team won't be long in matching it."

"I haven't seen Julie since Wednesday," Debbie Wright protested.

"You were at work all day? Someone can corroborate that?"

"Yes."

"Can you explain what happened to your car?" said Macpherson.

Debbie Wright didn't answer the question. Colin and Louise Cosgrove looked at the DS as though he had sprouted two heads.

"I had the car," said Daniel Wright. He picked up the broken stem of Louise Cosgrove's glass and sat beside his wife. He looked to his in-laws and then at her, his eyes imploring forgiveness. The face of a traitor.

"I had the car. I know why you're here."

Chapter 23

Veronica Taylor shook her head and rubbed her eyes.

"Yes. I'm looking at it now. He's going to go on record?" She moved the phone to her other ear and tapped Simpson on the shoulder. A gesture to hold what he was doing.

"That's something, I suppose. Are you two heading back?"

Taylor moved to the conference table and took an edge. She listened to Macpherson as she looked down at the doctor's evaluations and medical reports.

"No, don't bother. The two of you get home and get some sleep. We'll wrap up here and do the handover in the morning. The DPP needs his two breakfasts before he's firing on all cylinders. Cheers, Doc. Good job. Tell Erin I appreciate her putting up with you." Taylor gave a low chuckle and moved the phone from her ear to avoid the worst of the retort. She stood and moved nearer to her two DCs.

"You don't mean that. See you in the morning. Night."

She killed the call and peered past Cook at the report on Simpson's screen.

"Stabbed?" Cook edged her chair aside to give her inspector better access.

"Stabbed. Scalded. Burned and beaten." Simpson scrolled down the page. "Jesus, this makes grim reading."

Veronica Taylor looked at the wall-mounted screen. Jimmy

Harding hadn't moved, apart from to cross his wrists. His head hung low. His eyes remained focused on a spot on the table and Henry Scott seemed to have given up trying to engage him in conversation, preferring to scroll through his phone. He already had his jacket on, ready to sweep up the formalities to follow.

"How long does this go back?" she asked.

"Three years. Although the complaints weren't raised until the end of the relationship."

Simpson dragged and dropped the data. He added it to the print queue along with the preliminary reports Taylor had just requested from the Forensic team at Seapark.

"That doesn't explain why it didn't go anywhere. This level of abuse? Someone should have caught it." Cook looked from the screen to Taylor. "This is criminal."

"It is, Carrie." Taylor took a deep breath and straightened her jacket.

"Let's go and put an end to it. I want to make sure that little Tommy Cosgrove is the final innocent victim of this."

Chapter 24

Half a dozen electronic chirps. The dull clunk of the lock release and then click clack as it re-engaged.

Veronica Taylor took her seat, placing the evidence folder between herself and Carrie Cook. Cook, sitting sideways on her chair, teased her skirt hem down and then started the recording equipment.

"Interview resumes 1:47 A.M. Same persons present."

"Thanks, Carrie," said Taylor. She sat back and sighed.

"It's been a long day, Jimmy. Mr Scott here looks just about beat." She smiled. Henry Scott huffed a breath and checked the oversized dial of his wristwatch.

"I got it wrong," she said, leaning forward to rest her elbows on the table. "I'm not afraid to admit it. You had me more than once and nearly got away with it too. What I don't understand, Jimmy, is why you would do it?"

Jimmy Harding looked a beaten man. The first and second fingers of both hands had the nails bitten to the quick. His hair was dishevelled and Taylor could smell the fug of anxiety and stress.

He rubbed his forehead.

"Why? Why what? I keep telling you it was an accident."

"I see. OK. We'll do this my way then. Sam?" said Taylor.

Once again the PSNI logo dissolved to be replaced by two

scenes of holiday relaxation and a further two snapped on a boozy night out. The last showed a cozy picture of domestic bliss, partners wrapped in a blanket before a blazing log fire.

"Do you recognise the woman on the right, Jimmy?"

"What is this, Inspector?" Scott looked at the images then to his client with an expression of surprise.

"Well, do you recognise the woman?"

"Jeannette Burrows," said Harding.

"Jeannette Burrows. Pretty girl. I'd have given my right arm for those cheekbones when I was her age."

The girl's hair was similar to Taylor's in colour, although shorter, with the luminous sheen of a fresh horse chestnut. She was tanned, with dark eyes and a wide innocent smile. The only flaw was a series of angry scabs on the left arm which held up the camera for the selfie.

"Next image."

Scott flinched, a natural reaction when faced with the horrific contrast between the woman who had been and the woman who now was. Jeannette Burrow's hair, lacking the previous lustre, was scraped back from a pale, frightened face. Her dark eyes were haunted and ringed with angry bruising. Stitches marred the beauty, physical scars that would never heal and were a constant reminder of the psychological damage that she would never get over.

The brutal cuts severed the top lip and gouged a path upwards, slicing through the edge of the left nostril and leaving the apple of her cheek hanging in a loose flap of flesh.

"Brutal, isn't it?" said Taylor.

"Inspector, if you are pursuing this as an additional charge, I suggest you get the formalities out of the way first." Scott turned a few degrees in his seat to better avoid the image in his eye line.

"Are you going to tell him or am I?" Taylor sniffed, folding her hands on the table and searching the top of Harding's head, which faced her.

"Jimmy? I'll ask again. Look at that face up there and tell me why?"

Harding looked up. His face was twisted in pain and grief.

"She didn't mean it."

Taylor slid the folder to the centre of the table and flipped the cover.

"It goes back five years. When I read this and your records side by side I couldn't tell the difference. Did you ever meet Jeannette?"

A tear rolled down Harding's cheek.

"Once." His voice broke. "In town. I didn't know it was her at first. She'd a hood up. Had lost stones in weight. When she saw us I've never seen anyone so scared."

"Do you blame her?"

"Julie said…"

"What did Julie say to explain that?" Taylor snapped.

Harding put his hands over his eyes and shook his head.

"We didn't make the connection at first because she was going by her middle name when we investigated the initial complaints. Ruby, isn't it? I can see why. Suits her in that picture."

They all looked at the image of two young women lounging on a beach, one with glossy chestnut hair and the other with deep red curls. Arms and legs entwined. The look of adolescent love on the faces.

"Started innocuously enough. Trips and falls, minor accidents, and then it got more hot and heavy until Julie, Ruby, did that."

"Julie didn't mean it. She's ill…" Jimmy Harding paused. The narrowing of Taylor's eyes dared him to follow through with an excuse for the barbarity.

"Is that why you put up with it? Because she has a sickness? Depression? Aggression? Psychopathy?"

"No."

"Sam?"

The images changed to a set of bottles and a slide of finger-print analysis.

"These are on the fly, but we'll have them ironclad for the jury."

"What's this?" asked the solicitor.

"Twenty-one spirit bottles recovered in Mr Harding's outhouse," said Cook.

"Julie is an alcoholic and a violent abuser, isn't she, Jimmy?"

"No."

"Image Charlie, zero one. A shattered wine bottle. The prints around the neck are those of Julie Cosgrove. The blood on the pointy end is Jimmy's," said Taylor. Scott's surprise reached his hairline.

"No!" Harding swept the file off the table, tears of frustration and shame flowing.

"Jimmy, we have a witness."

"No."

"Daniel Wright was at your house today. He saw what happened."

"No." Jimmy Harding pushed back from the table.

"These are the preliminary forensic findings on the weapon discharge. Your prints are on the weapon. Your clothes are covered in gunshot residue and blood. Sam?"

The image on the screen changed to Harding's shotgun in the lab, with arrows, diamonds and text boxes transposed on top.

"You grabbed the barrel. You were trying to disarm her. That's what happened. She had been drinking. She lost control again, but this time hitting you a slap or coming at you with a bottle wouldn't be good enough."

Jimmy Harding leapt to his feet. His breath heaving in

panic.

"Freddie Moore had been winding her up, telling her you and Connie were carrying on behind her back again. She took the bait."

"She didn't…"

"Sit down, Jimmy."

Harding paced the room, fists balled.

"Jimmy. It's not your fault. You don't need to keep it hidden any more," said Taylor.

"Jimmy. Is this true?" Scott stood, hands up to pacify his cornered and defeated client.

"It was an accident," Harding screamed.

"Jimmy, come on. Sit down. Tell me. You don't have to be afraid any more. Do it for Tommy. Tell the truth for him." Taylor's voice was calm.

Harding swayed. He put his hands against the wall to steady himself. The colour drained from his face.

Taylor stood. Cook reached for the panic button.

"I'm OK," he mumbled.

"Sit down. It's all right." Taylor took him by the arm and eased him back into the seat. Cook removed her fingers from the button. Scott shifted his seat a little closer.

"I'm sorry," Harding said, the anguish cracking his voice. His eyes were raw, his mouth twisted in grief and pain.

"You don't need to be sorry, Jimmy. It's over. She can't hurt you now."

Epilogue

"I still can't believe it." Sam Simpson stared at the holiday image of Julie Cosgrove. A large glass with straw and customary umbrella. A carefree smile. Wind in her hair.

"You never know what goes on behind closed doors, Sam," said Taylor.

Simpson blew out a breath, gave a half shake, half nod of his head and pointed at the monitor.

"What will happen to him?"

"Hopefully he'll get the help he deserves. Family liaison will take over. Now the abuse is out in the open, if he keeps talking his GP will refer him to the proper bodies for help. It's tragic, right enough," said Taylor.

"What about her?"

"She's going nowhere. Her mother will kick up a storm, but as long as the son-in-law stands by his statement, it's cut and dry. He was at the house at the behest of his wife to pick up some bags Julie had promised to her earlier in the week. Heard the argument and saw her brandishing the shotgun. To let Harding take the wrap for it was probably more for the sake of his wife and mother-in-law than any affinity he had to Julie. I'll speak with the DPP in the morning and see how he wants to pursue the formal charge against Julie. Then we wait for Diane Pearson's final evidence reports from the scene."

"To shoot your own kid, though."

"She needs help as much as Jimmy Harding. Has to if she was going down the road of murder-suicide." Taylor looked at the two young women in the picture. A glimpse at what might have been.

"Maybe her family didn't approve of the relationship with Jeannette. Julie vented her frustrations on her. Eventually she bowed to family pressure and took up with the first fella that came along."

The age-old tale of hurting the ones you love. Burying the truth. Denial and repression building to aggression and a point of explosive release.

"When she fell pregnant and then moved out to the cottage, her mother started again. Julie might have been using the drink to cope with the guilt or because she's turned her back on a different life to please her family and now they still weren't happy. Behind that smiling face, Julie Cosgrove is a very sad and very angry woman. She's ill, Sam."

The image of the happy family lay amid the chaos of the observation room conference table. The gap-toothed smile of a little boy was a harrowing reminder of the tragedy that had struck a picture-postcard cottage in the windswept fields overlooking the sleeping city.

On the monitor, Cook led Harding and Scott from the interview room to appear on the landing lobby camera, where a uniform PC waited. She shook hands with both and spoke a few words to Harding. Sympathies and best wishes. Taylor watched the broken man give a solemn nod. Scott led the way as solicitor and client followed the officer down the stairs, each in their own thoughts as they took the short walk down a few floors to the rear parking bay.

"You did good today, Sam."

"Thanks Guv," said Simpson. He spun his chair round. "I appreciate it." He bowed his head. "Lesson learned. First instincts can be wrong. I'm sorry about that." He gave a grateful smile.

"They can be right, too. We just can't let ourselves be blinded to other possibilities. You did good."

The door access code chirped and Cook entered. The scattered evidence was restored to order under her arm. She kicked a small wooden wedge into place, holding the door open for the room to air and for ease of wheeling the requisitioned files back down to central records.

"You too, Carrie. Thanks. It's been a long day. I appreciate the effort. Take a few extra hours in the morning. I'll get the paperwork vetted for the DPP on Julie Cosgrove."

Both DCs expressed their thanks.

"If you ever want to escape the dark side, Sam, I could use you."

"Leave Inspector MacDonald?"

Taylor laughed.

"You hoping he'll bring you back a set of maracas?"

"No. I appreciate it, but I thought you had a new start coming on?"

"I don't know what you're encouraging them for. They're only doing their bloody job." A gruff voice caught them unawares. Taylor turned to the door with a smile for the red face that entered.

"They need to get that flaming lift fixed." Doc Macpherson bustled into the room with a six pack of cola under one arm and a carrier bag hanging in his big fist. "What? Did you think us two have been running round the countryside all day for you lot to steal the bloody glory from under us?"

"Can you transfer me instead?" said Erin Reilly, another fat carrier bag clutched in her hand.

"Aye. Ronnie, I need to have a word with you about this one. Insults. Insolence. Insubordination..." Macpherson dropped the bag onto the table.

"If I go to HR with a complaint from you they'll laugh me out of the station."

"What's all this?" Cook sidled over. She rustled a finger in the carrier bag. "Indian? Doc, I don't care what they say about you. They have you all wrong. Is that pakora?" She nudged her DS.

"The Maharaja was open so we… I say we, but it was my idea." He winked at Taylor.

"For God's sake." Reilly rolled her eyes and ripped open the carrier. "Never listen to him. Help yourselves. There's enough here to feed the station. Slick, what do you fancy?"

Taylor watched the group huddle around the cartons and debate what looked best. She felt famished but had no appetite. She was wrung out after the day and her mind was still occupied with Jimmy Harding and the days, weeks and months he was about to face. Hopefully, with whatever friendship he had with Connie Moore and the support of the Dereks, he would come through the ordeal. She scooped up the family picture. A last look at the smiling face of a little boy whose life was cut far too short. The next time she would see him he would be on Professor Thompson's slab.

Reilly was dishing out. Cook had a palm full of tandoori pakora and was laughing from behind her free hand as Macpherson protested against Reilly's refusal to heap another spoonful of biryani chicken onto his naan. The playful banter of the team washed over her. Macpherson smiled and held up a tin of cola.

Taylor closed the file.

"I swear I don't know where you put it. You haven't rested your jaws all day," said Reilly.

Taylor accepted the can from Macpherson's big hand. His eyes wrinkled in mirth. As he opened his mouth to speak she cut across to answer for him.

"You know you can't fatten a thoroughbred, Erin."

Afterword

THANK-YOU FOR READING 'BEHIND CLOSED DOORS'

I sincerely hope you enjoyed this Novella Case-File. If you can **please** spare a moment to leave a short review it will be very much appreciated and helps immensely in assisting others to find this, and my other books.

You can leave your review here

Follow Detective Inspector Veronica Taylor and her team in my Debut novel:

'CODE OF SILENCE'

You can find out about this book and more in the series by signing up at my website:

www.pwjordanauthor.com

Get Exclusive Material

About Phillip Jordan

ABOUT PHILLIP JORDAN

Phillip Jordan was born in Belfast, Northern Ireland and grew up in the city that holds the dubious double honour of being home to Europe's Most Bombed Hotel and scene of its largest ever bank robbery.

He had a successful career in the Security Industry for twenty years before transitioning into the Telecommunications Sector.

Aside from writing Phillip has competed in Olympic and Ironman Distance Triathlon events both Nationally and Internationally including a European Age-Group Championship and the World Police and Fire Games.

Taking the opportunity afforded by recent world events to write full-time Phillip wrote his Debut Crime Thriller, CODE OF SILENCE, finding inspiration in the dark and tragic history of Northern Ireland but also in the black humour, relentless tenacity and Craic of the people who call the fabulous but flawed City of his birth home.

Phillip now lives on the County Down coast and is currently writing two novel series.

For more information:

www.pwjordanauthor.com
www.facebook.com / phillipjordanauthor /

Copyright

* * *

FIVE FOUR PUBLISHING

Printed in Great Britain
by Amazon